By Pat & Sandy Roy
Adapted by John J. Horn

Adapted from the Exciting Audio Adventure
The Adventure Begins

2

November 2014

Creation Works
P.O. Box 2128 El Cajon, CA 92021
www.jonathanpark.com

ISBN 978-1-941510-32-2

Cover Design by Austin Collins, My Hero Media
Original typography by Justin Turley
Updated typogrophy by Austin Collins, My Hero Media

Printed in the United States of America.

Table of Contents

Introduction

Since 1998, the Jonathan Park radio drama series has delighted thousands of children (and adults) with exciting family stories that honor God as the Creator of this world and leave listeners waiting breathless for the next adventure.

Now, all the drama of Jonathan Park rests in your own two hands.

In *Jonathan Park: A New Beginning* you will read the novel version of radio episodes five through eight. Join the Park and Brenan families as they tackle obstacles in their exciting journey to building the creation museum.

Read and re-read your favorite parts, find new scenes not included in the radio drama episodes, and immerse yourself in the world of Jonathan Park as you live life through his eyes. Each episode offers compelling evidence for creation and ways to refute evolution—not because the Bible needs to be proved, but because as Christians, it's our job to be "always be ready to give a defense" for the hope within us.

This is our Father's world. God created it. We can explore it. So live the adventure!

Disaster at Brenan Bluff

For many months, a small team of diggers had been looking for a dinosaur graveyard at Brenan Ranch in Abiquiu, fifty miles north of Santa Fe, New Mexico. On a cool Monday morning, paleontologist Dr. Kendall Park and Jim Brenan sped toward the dig site in a red 4x4 truck.

Dr. Park was wearing a Fedora and grinned as he swung the truck around the worst ruts and bounced over the shallower ones.

"Kendall, what are we doing?" Mr. Brenan asked. He was smiling too, but in a confused sort of way.

"Jim, have I got something to show you!"

"This is something good, isn't it?"

Dr. Park roared into the temporary dig site and killed the engine. "Remember when we first discovered that dinosaur fossil in the hidden cave? I couldn't help but think we might find more somewhere else on your ranch."

Mr. Brenan nodded slowly. "Yes, that's why we hired people to help you excavate. So, what is it?"

Dr. Park threw his door open. "Get out and take a look for yourself!"

About a dozen workers in hardhats and orange safety vests were scattered at the base of the cliffs, most wielding shovels and pickaxes. A Bobcat beeped as it backed away from a pile of dirt.

One of the workers waved at Dr. Park as he and Mr. Brenan approached. "Sir, we've found another one over here!"

Mr. Brenan looked at Dr. Park. "What's going on?"

"We've found a dinosaur graveyard!" Dr. Park wanted to fling his hat into the air, but it didn't seem very professional. He grabbed Jim's shoulders instead. "A few days ago we moved closer to the cliffs, and since then we've found many more *Coelophysis* fossils."

"Thank God!" Mr. Brenan exclaimed. "We've got our dream!"

"Not only will we be able to build our museum, but we'll be able to provide the public with a view of a real dinosaur graveyard as it's being excavated!"

Something rumbled high above them. Dr. Park jerked to look up at the cliff. He gasped. A load of rocks was tumbling down the cliff-face.

"Run!" one of the workers yelled. "Get away from the cliffs!"

The workers dropped their tools and raced for the open space, their hands clamped over their hard hats. Dr. Park and Mr. Brenan sprinted for the cars. Kendall thought about his Fedora—it wouldn't protect his head from a falling rock very well.

They reached the cars breathless, but safe. The rumbling had stopped and the landslide seemed to be over, but the cliffs still looked unsteady. A pile of boulders lay near the dig site. Several of the rocks had bounced into the work area.

"Is everyone all right?" Dr. Park asked.

Joe, the foreman, counted the men off on his fingers. "Yes,

sir, we're all okay."

"Those cliffs look badly eroded," Mr. Brenan said.

The spot where most of the rockslide had come from was a darker red than the rest of the cliff, as it hadn't been baked by the sun. The rock-layers surrounding the new cleft looked unstable.

"It's probably from that terrible storm we had last year," Joe said. "Do you guys remember? This whole area was flooded."

Mr. Brenan coughed. "Oh, I seem to remember something about a flood, how about you, Kendall?"

Dr. Park smiled and shrugged. "I was in the dark over the whole thing—like a cave." He grew more serious as he studied the cliff-face. "If those cliffs collapse, we may lose the whole graveyard."

Jonathan Park dashed into his classroom with a group of boys.

"King of four-square—Jonathan Park!" he announced. He sat down, panting. Four-square under a middle-of-the-day New Mexico sun was draining.

The science teacher, Mr. Benefucio, walked between the desks, calming kids and making sure that everyone settled back into their correct seats. "Okay, okay, I hope everyone had a very fulfilling recess."

Eddie stuck his hand up. "Mr. Benefucio, I personally think that recess provides us with an excellent chance for socialization and the opportunity to rehearse our future roles in society."

The class tittered at his mock solemnity. He sounded like Calvin from the Calvin and Hobbes comic strip on one of the days he was trying to act good.

Mr. Benefucio smiled. "Thank you for that insightful editorial, Edward. We will now proceed with the learning phase of your education." He reached his desk and turned around. "I've cleverly devised a project that combines a history assignment with our science lesson. What I'd like all of you to do is write a report on a great scientist of the past."

Thad raised his hand. "Like Isaac Newton?"

"Yes, Thad."

"I could do the report on my dad!" Jonathan said.

Somebody at the back of the room laughed. It was Rusty, the class bully, who had fiery red hair, a long nose, big fists, and a nasty personality.

"That certainly fits the assignment," Rusty said. "After all, your dad really is a scientist of the past."

Jonathan clenched the edge of his des, whipped his head around and stared at Rusty. "What do you mean by that?"

"I heard your dad got fired from a museum in Montana."

Jonathan scowled. "My dad is the best scientist that has ever walked the face of the earth! And that's where I got my brains—too bad for you."

Mr. Benefucio rapped his desk. "Okay, that's enough."

But Rusty wasn't finished. "You always think you're so much better than everyone else." He glared at Jonathan.

Mr. Benefucio's voice hardened into punishment mode. Everyone in class knew that tone. "Okay, Rusty, I'll see you after class tomorrow for detention. And Jonathan, you're one step away, my friend. Got it?"

Jonathan sighed. "Yes, sir."

Dr. Park parked his truck and walked into his home slowly, twirling his Fedora in his hand. Mrs. Park greeted him at the door.

"How was your day?" she asked.

Dr. Park tried to smile. "Angela, we found a dinosaur graveyard!"

"Well—congratulations!" Mrs. Park's eyebrows narrowed. "So, why the long face?"

Dr. Park tossed his Fedora onto the couch and sat down next to it. He steepled his fingers for a moment, thinking about the problem at the dig site. "The cliffs above the site are unstable, and we're afraid they may collapse on the graveyard."

Dr. Park's phone rang. "Wait a minute, Honey, I'll be right back." He dug his cellphone out of his jeans pocket and walked into the next room. "Hello, this is Dr. Kendall Park."

A man was on the other end. "Hello, Dr. Park, my name is Sherman Bott. I'm a creationist here in Santa Fe."

Sherman Bott. The name wasn't familiar.

"So what can I do for you, Mr. Bott?" Dr. Park asked.

"Actually, I was hoping that you would help me make the case for creation. You see, last week I was on a local talk radio show. It was horrible. The host made the claim that there aren't any real scientists who believe in creation. He was so confident that he challenged me to come back on this Wednesday at three-thirty to prove him wrong. Dr. Park, I heard you're a Ph.D. vertebrate paleontologist. Would you be willing to go on the program with me?"

Dr. Park scratched his chin. It sounded like a good opportunity to present the creation message. Three-thirty on Wednesday? He should be able to make it. "Sure, I'll do it, Sherman. Would you mind if I brought my son with me?"

"That would be fine. Maybe we can even let him sit in with you."

Jonathan, Jessie, and the rest of the Eagle's Nest Gang sat in the Parks' living room with Grandpa Benjamin. A plate of chocolate chip cookies and a carton of milk sat on the coffee table.

"Grandpa, thanks for taking the time to help us with our report," Jonathan said.

"Yeah, thank you, Mr. Park," Thad echoed.

Eddie performed a sitting bow with clasped hands. "Mr. Park, you're great. Without you, this would be impossible!"

Grandpa Benjamin chuckled. "My pleasure, boys."

Mike groaned from one of the armchairs. "I can't believe I'm here. I'm not even doing a report."

"Me too," piped Timmy.

Jessie shrugged. "Just because we're not in Mr. Benefucio's class doesn't mean we can't learn something."

Mike rolled his eyes. "You're just saying that because you homeschoolers love word."

"Mike," Grandpa Benjamin said, "Jessie just enjoys learning new things. But back to our subject. Did you guys know that some of the best scientists in all of history believed in the Creator?"

"Like who?" Timmy asked.

"Well, possibly one of the most famous was Isaac Newton. He was an astronomer who lived from—what was it—I think 1642 to 1727. One of his great accomplishments was to develop the type of math known as calculus."

"Oh." Eddie snapped his fingers. "So he's the one to blame."

"He was also the inventor of the first reflecting telescope, and he studied the motions of our solar system. But he's most famous for the discovery of gravity."

Thad cocked an eyebrow. "You mean they didn't know that things always fall down before Newton?"

Grandpa Benjamin laughed. "No, they knew things fell, they just didn't have a theory to explain why. Newton was a genius. He also believed that God created this world. He once said, 'this most beautiful system of the sun, planets, and comets could only proceed from the counsel and dominion of an intelligent and powerful Being.'"

Eddie tapped his milk glass with his fingernail. "Hey, what about the guy who invented milk?"

Mike snorted. "Eddie, it comes out of cows—no one invented it."

"But the guy's name is on this carton," Eddie said, pointing to the small container of milk on the table.

Grandpa Benjamin smiled. "That's Louis Pasteur. He's the one who invented the process we call 'pasteurization.'"

"What's that?" Timmy asked.

"It's the process that takes harmful bacteria out of milk." Grandpa Benjamin poured himself a glass and held it out for inspection. "The milk we buy at the store, like this milk, is not straight from a cow's udder. You see, Louis Pasteur was the one who identified several harmful bacteria, and made vaccines to cure them—harmful diseases like rabies, diphtheria, and anthrax." Grandpa Benjamin sipped his milk. "Thousands of people owe their lives to the work done by Pasteur."

"So what exactly did he do?" Thad asked.

"Before Pasteur was born, people believed that if you left meat out to rot, maggots would form—or if you left out dirty rags that it would make mice. They thought this because they always found maggots in rotten meat, and mice in places they kept dirty rags. During Pasteur's time, evolutionists liked the idea of life coming from non-living objects, because it meant that life could form without God."

"But that's not true—is it?" Timmy asked.

"No, and Pasteur proved it. He did a series of experiments that proved the scientific law that says that life can only come from life."

"That seems pretty simple," Thad said. "I thought

everybody knew that."

"Well, they do now." Grandpa Benjamin set down his glass. "That scientific law has never been broken—no one has ever seen life come from anything but another living creature. Pasteur's experiments dealt a serious blow to evolution."

Eddie dipped another chocolate chip cookie in his milk and took a big bite. "I never thought of milk as a proof for creation. Maybe Mom will let me drink more now. How does all of this hurt evolution?"

"Well, evolutionists say the universe started with a Big Bang that formed planet Earth, and then somehow a single-celled organism came to life in the ocean. But that's just as silly as saying that mice come from dirty rags. It violates this law of science—that life can only come from life."

"So Louis Pasteur must have believed in a Creator?" Jonathan said.

"Absolutely. He once said, 'the more I study nature, the more I stand amazed at the work of the Creator.'"

Jessie spoke. "My dad also told me about Robert Boyle."

Grandpa Benjamin nodded. "Ah, yes. He was the founder of modern chemistry, and well-known for speaking about the Bible."

Dr. and Mrs. Park came into the living room and smiled at the group.

"Quite the party in here," Dr. Park said.

Jonathan leaned back in his seat and propped his feet on the coffee table. Some days it just felt good to be alive, and today, he felt super proud of how important his dad was.

"Dad, you're going to go down in history as one of the best paleontologists ever. We'll be famous!"

"Jonathan—"

"It's so cool to have a special family," Jonathan said.

Timmy frowned. "Well—my dad is a state police officer."

Jonathan waved his hand. "That's nice, Timmy, but that's

nothing like having a world-famous paleontologist for a dad."

"Jonathan!" his mom exclaimed.

Jonathan looked up quickly. Neither of his parents looked happy. Was something wrong? "But, Mom, that's why the radio station wants us to be on the air."

"All right, young man, that's enough," Dr. Park said.

Jonathan gulped. Now what had he done?

Grandpa Benjamin looked at Dr. Park. "Son, what's all this about?"

Dr. Park sighed. "There's a talk show host claiming that real scientists can't believe in creation."

"Well, I was just pointing out to the kids that many of the founding fathers of science believed in the Creator."

Eddie frowned. "It's too bad you couldn't bring a few of them back to life so they could go on the radio with you. And, I'd interview them for my report."

"Hey! That's an idea!" Dr. Park said.

Eddie jumped up. "You know how to bring them back to life?"

"Hmm? Oh, no, I didn't mean that, but why not invite some *living* creation scientists to be on the radio with me?"

"That's an excellent idea," Grandpa Benjamin said.

The excitement fell away from Dr. Park's face. "Unfortunately, I don't know any. Ever since I became a creationist, I've been the Lone Ranger."

Mrs. Park patted his shoulder. "Well, maybe this is your chance to get plugged in!"

"I think you're right. Let me talk to Sherman and see if he has any other contacts. Oh, and Angela, I think you need to have a talk with Jonathan."

Jonathan followed his mom to his room. He found himself counting the rows of flowers on the wallpaper as they walked down the hall. Judging by his mom's face and his dad's tone, this conversation wasn't going to be easy.

Mrs. Park sat Jonathan on his bed and stood by the door, her arms crossed. "Jonathan, I heard the way you were bragging about going on the talk show."

Jonathan gulped. "I was just excited that Dad and I get to be on the radio in front of everyone."

"In front of everyone?" Mrs. Park frowned. "Jonathan, what are your motives? Are you going just so you can be a star, or are you interested in why the Lord has given you this opportunity?"

Jonathan wound a loose thread from his shirt around his right index finger. "I didn't mean anything bad. . . ."

"Yes, but Jonathan, God says He hates our pride. And sadly, our pride can oftentimes hurt others. Think about how the other boys felt when you said your dad is better than theirs."

Jonathan hadn't thought about that possibility. Come to think of it, Timmy had looked a little offended. And Mike.

"In Proverbs 16:18 it says: 'Pride goes before destruction, and a haughty spirit before a fall.' Jonathan, the Bible says that if you are prideful, you will fall."

"I guess talking big makes me feel like I'm okay," Jonathan said.

"Jonathan, you're already someone special—you're the child of the Creator. But when we build ourselves up, our attention is on us, not on Him."

"I know."

"Whenever you feel prideful, stop and remember to focus on Him."

Jonathan nodded. "I'll try." He wished it was as easy as it sounded.

His mom unfolded her arms. "For now, we better tell Grandpa that it's time to break up the study session. If your father is going to show you and the gang the dinosaur graveyard tomorrow, we all need a good night's sleep."

Kendall double-checked the number on his cellphone's screen with the number on the paper in front of him. They matched. He pressed 'call' and held the phone to his ear.

"Hello?" answered a deep voice.

"Hi, I'm looking for Dr. Humphreys."

"Russ Humphreys speaking."

"Hello, Dr. Humphreys, my name is Dr. Kendall Park. I'm a Ph.D. vertebrate paleontologist here in Santa Fe and I got your number from Sherman Bott. You're a physicist, from what I understand?"

"Yes, that's right."

"Would you mind telling me what areas you specialize in?"

Dr. Humphreys cleared his throat. "Well, I'm a physicist at Sandia National Laboratories, and I've done nuclear physics, geophysics, pulse-power research, theoretical atomic and nuclear physics. I also worked on the particle-beam fusion project."

Dr. Park raised his eyebrows. This was definitely one of the men he was looking for. "Wow, I'm impressed," he said. "Dr. Humphreys, I've recently been invited to be on a talk show. The host has been claiming that no real scientists believe in creation. Would you consider calling in during the program?"

Dr. Humphreys hesitated for a moment. "Sure, Kendall, I'll be happy to call in, but I've never done radio before."

"Don't worry. All I'm asking for is a brief call, to give your name and areas of scientific expertise. Lord willing, we'll have a number of creation scientists from different fields doing the same."

The next day, the Parks, Brenans, and the Eagle's Nest Gang drove to the dig site on Brenan Ranch. The construction workers had all been given a couple days off until an engineer could look at the cliff and give a recommendation.

The group gathered near the Bobcat, where two fossils were halfway through the excavation process.

"Look at all these!" Thad said.

"This graveyard is so neat!" Timmy turned to look up at the cliff.

Mrs. Brenan was also looking up at the cliff, but she didn't look impressed. "Okay everyone, let's stay back from the cliffs."

"You're right, Martha," Mr. Brenan agreed. "They're still very dangerous."

Shadow, the Brenan's dog, eyed the dinosaur bones expectantly. Mr. Brenan rubbed his ears. "Sorry boy, those bones are a little too valuable for you."

Thad turned to Dr. Park. "Dr. Park, studying fossils seems pretty awesome—do you like it?"

"I love it. I get to see first hand the evidence that the Creator has left behind. Ever since I was just old enough to pronounce the word, I've wanted to be a paleontologist. And now that I'm a Christian, it's more fulfilling than I had ever dreamed."

"Dad, are you the only creation paleontologist?" Jonathan asked.

His dad laughed. "Sometimes it feels that way, but did you know, one of the first paleontologists was a creationist? His name was John Woodward. He lived in the late 1600s and died around 1728. He was the man who started the science of looking for fossils and trying to understand what creatures left them behind."

"You said he believed in creation?" Mr. Brenan asked.

"Yes, and listen to this—he believed the reason for so many fossils in the ground was a direct result of Noah's Flood. Just like our dinosaur graveyard—it shows evidence of a great flood."

Shadow started barking furiously and dashed toward the cliff.

"Look, it's a rabbit!" Mike said.

Jessie called Shadow to come back, but he was too focused on his mission to notice, so she ran after him. They were both running straight for the cliff.

Mr. Brenan cupped his hands. "Jessie, don't go any closer!"

"I'll get her," Jonathan said. He started running after her.

Something rumbled.

Eddie put his hand to his ear. "Uh, guys, something is grumbling, and that's *not* my stomach."

"Rocks!" Mike yelled. Jonathan looked up. There was a gash in the cliff where the first rock slide happened its red coloring less faded than the surrounding rocks. The rocks at the bottom of the fresh cleft were crumbling. Shadow's barking was causing another slide.

"Get out of there!" Dr. Park yelled.

Jonathan was already too close to the cliffs to escape the slide. Jessie turned, her face twisted with horror.

"Jonathan!"

"Jessie!"

There was a narrow trench in the dirt, parallel to the cliff, from one of the excavations. Jonathan grabbed Jessie and pulled her into it. He was still face up, looking into a sky full of falling debris. The trench was too narrow for him to turn his head quickly, so he squeezed his eyes shut, covered his face with his hands, and prayed.

There was grinding, and crashing, and enormous thuds all around, while the ground trembled like mattress springs under a jumping kid. The little bit of light he sensed from under his closed eyelids was quickly blotted out. Then everything was quiet.

Jonathan opened his eyes. A huge chunk of rock straddled the trench four inches above his nose. He blinked the settling dust away from his eyes and took a slow, cautious breath. Dirt particles clung to his throat and set him coughing violently. Little bits of light sneaked under the edges of the rock.

"Jessie?" he whispered, trying to keep his lips as narrow as possible to stop the dirt from getting in. "Jessie?"

"I'm—over here." Her voice was weak. It came from the other side of the boulder.

Jonathan tried to move his legs, but they wouldn't budge. *Broken?* No, they didn't hurt. They were trapped under the rock.

"Are you okay?" Jonathan whispered.

"It's hard—to breathe. It's really—tight—on my chest."

"Jessie! Jonathan!"

Jonathan could faintly here the voices and footsteps of the group.

"Dad! Mr. Brenan! Down here!" Jonathan yelled.

Dr. Park's shadow blocked even more of the light that was seeping through the rock. "They're under this boulder," Dr. Park said. His voice was close, but deadened by the stone. "Let's rock it to the left so we can get Jessie out, then we'll move it back the other way for Jonathan. On three! One—"

"We're coming, Jessie!" Mr. Brenan yelled.

"Two—"

Both men grunted. "Three!"

Jonathan screamed. The rock was squeezing his right shinbone like a nut in a nutcracker.

"Stop!" Dr. Park yelled. The rock dropped back into place, and the worst of the pressure was relieved. "Jonathan, what's wrong?"

"My leg—when you moved the rock." Jonathan squeezed

his eyes shut, trying to stop the tears. He was trapped. It was like being buried alive. The skin on his back tingled.

"Okay," Mr. Brenan said, "then let's rock it to the right so we can get Jonathan, and then back the other way for Jessie."

The pressure lightened—another few inches and Jonathan could move his leg.

Jessie gasped. "Dad—I can't breathe!"

"The rock is pushing against her chest!" Mr. Brenan said.

The rock dropped back into place and a little ridge jabbed into the thin layer of skin on Jonathan's shinbone.

"Now what are we going to do?" Dr. Park said. His voice was shaky with tension. "If we rock it one way, we'll break Jonathan's leg—if we go the other way, we'll crush Jessie."

Jessie was breathing in crisp gasps. That rock needed to come off *now*.

Jonathan gulped. There were only two ways out of this, and one of them was over his leg. It had to be done.

"Break my leg."

"What?" Jonathan's dad got down so that his mouth was close to the cracks where the light came in. "Son?"

"Push the rock on my leg. We need to get Jessie out *now*."

"Son—I can't do this to you."

"Dad, it's the only way to save Jessie."

Mr. Brenan's voice trembled. "Kendall, I could never ask you to hurt your own son."

Jessie's gasps were quicker and shorter.

Jonathan clenched his hands. "Dad, there's no other way. You've got to do it!"

Dr. Park's voice was husky. "I love you, Son! Okay, Jim—on three. One—" the boulder started rocking. "Two—" the weight jammed into Jonathan's right shinbone like a corkscrew. One more push—

"Wait!" Dr. Park said. "What am I thinking? Boys, I have some two-by-fours in the back of the truck. Run and get them, quick!"

The dads were propping up the rock as best they could, so that Jessie could breathe a little easier. If it slipped down any farther on Jonathan's leg—he shivered at the thought.

Jonathan counted every second that the Eagle's Nest was gone. It was nineteen—only nineteen?

"We found six boards," Mike called.

Dr. Park's voice was still close to the crack. "Quick everyone, wedge an end under the rock. We don't have the strength to lift it, but if we use these two-by-fours as a lever, we'll be able to topple the rock down this pile of rubble."

The boards scraped against the rock as they were wedged into nooks and crannies.

"Push!"

Jonathan opened his eyes. For a moment, nothing happened, then slowly, very slowly, the light increased. The boulder was lifting. It kept rising, and soon Jonathan saw a glimpse of the sky above. The rock teetered on the edge. Another push—

The boulder rolled down, gouging a deep furrow in the pile of debris. Jonathan and Jessie were free.

Jonathan lay, dazed, now that the danger was gone. Hands grabbed his shoulders and pulled him out of the trench. He blinked in the sunlight. Jessie was already out and sitting on a rock with her parents kneeling next to her.

"I'm okay," Jessie said. My chest is just a little sore."

Jonathan bent down to brush the dirt off his pants. A little cloud of dust settled over the gravel. He smiled vaguely. "My leg is fine." He looked up at everyone. "Thanks to you guys."

"Hello, this is Dr. John Baumgardner."

"Hello Dr. Baumgardner, this is Dr. Kendall Park—I'm a

creationist here in New Mexico." Kendall switched his cellphone to his left hand and grabbed a pen. "I got your name from Dr. Humphreys. He says you accept the literal account of Genesis?"

"That is correct."

Dr. Park leaned back in his office chair and crossed his legs. "Can you tell me a little bit about yourself?"

"Well, for the last twenty-five years I've been very interested in the mechanism responsible for the Genesis Flood. I got a Ph.D. in geophysics to be able to work on this problem at a professional level. I've been a scientist in the theoretical division of Los Alamos National Laboratory. And I've been able to do a great deal of work in modeling, using some of the available super computers to model this catastrophe—a large tectonic catastrophe that I believe completely resurfaced the planet Earth in a very short period of time."

"I feel the same way," Dr. Park said. "Dr. Baumgardner, tomorrow I'm going to be on a nation-wide talk show. The host has been claiming that there are no scientists who believe in creation. Would you be willing to call in?"

"Sure, I'd be pleased to do that."

Dr. Park checked Dr. Baumgardner's name off on the list in his notebook. That was check number ten. Lord willing, Dr. Park was going to be with a very surprised talk show host tomorrow.

Jonathan stood facing the rest of his class three pages of double-spaced paper in his hands. He was on the last paragraph and still flub-free.

"I just want to finish by explaining why I chose Wernher von Braun for my report. Although I thought it was really neat that he designed the rocket that put man on the moon, it really meant a lot to me that he believed in the Creator. While most people know him for his achievements during his time as the director of NASA's Marshall Space Flight Center, few know about his faith in God."

Somebody in the back of the class snickered. Jonathan cleared his throat loudly and continued.

"Wernher von Braun once said, 'I find it as difficult to understand a scientist who does not acknowledge the presence of a superior rationality behind the existence of the universe as it is to comprehend a theologian who would deny the advances of science.' The world experienced a great loss when Dr. von Braun died in 1977." Jonathan folded his papers. "And that's my report. Thank you."

Mr. Benefucio led the class in a round of applause. "Good work, Jonathan," he said warmly.

Jonathan smiled. "Thanks. Since I come from a scientific family, I had a natural grip on the subject—that's why it really came together so well."

Mr. Benefucio coughed slightly. "Jonathan, remember, one should practice humility."

Jonathan thought of his talk with his mom. His chest deflated a little. "Yes, sir, I'm sorry."

One of the girls, Elizabeth, raised her hand. "I have a question. It's not exactly about your report, Jonathan, but about creation. The Bible says that God has always been around, but how can that be scientifically proven?"

"Well, Elizabeth—"Jonathan paused. How could you prove God scientifically? He gulped, and he felt his cheeks getting hot. "Um—well—Elizabeth, I'm not really sure."

"Hey," Rusty said, "you stumped the know-it-all!"

The recess bell rang.

Mr. Benefucio smiled. "Saved by the bell. After recess we'll hear Edward's report. Eddie, who is your report about?"

"Samuel Morse, the creationist who invented the telegraph."

"All right, everyone be back in fifteen minutes."

Rusty and another one of the tough kids, Spike, came out of class together and headed for the playground.

"Hey Rusty," Spike said, "you gonna pound that kid Jonathan at recess?"

"Naw." Rusty smirked. "I've got a better plan. You know how Jonathan has been bragging how he and his 'scientist' dad are gonna be on a talk show tomorrow? I'm going to call in and make him look like a fool."

"How you gonna do that?"

"Did you see how easily Elizabeth stumped him? He had no clue how to answer her." Rusty winked. "What would happen if he got asked the same question on *national* radio? He'd start babbling like a monkey. He'd look like a fool."

It was Wednesday. Kendall Park stood in the Brenans' kitchen, finishing a few details before heading to the radio station. Martha Brenan walked into the kitchen with a load of grocery bags.

"Hey, Kendall. I sure hope your wife didn't mind watching Jessie while I was running errands in Los Alamos."

"Are you kidding?" Dr. Park grinned. "Angela loves spending time with Jessie! They probably went to the mall or something. Besides, now Jessie can ride over to the radio station with Jonathan."

The home phone rang.

"Hello?" Mrs. Brenan looked at Dr. Park. "Yes, actually, he is here. I'll get him." She clapped her hand over the receiver. "It's for you."

"Interesting." Dr. Park took the phone. "Hello, Dr. Park speaking."

"This is Dr. Danny Faulkner," a man said. "I was just talking to Russ Humphreys, and he told me you were looking for some creation scientists to help you out on some sort of radio program?"

"Wow, your timing is perfect. Did you just try calling my house?"

"Yes, and your daughter gave me this number."

"Perfect." Dr. Park looked at his watch. He could probably squeeze a couple minutes in before he had to scram. "I was actually just about to head on over to the radio studio. Can you briefly tell me about yourself?" he asked.

"Sure," Dr. Faulkner said. "I'm an astronomer—I have a Ph.D. in astronomy. And I'm a professor at the University of South Carolina, Lancaster, where I teach astronomy and physics. And I'm one of just a small number of creation astronomers today in the world."

"So, you're a young earth creationist?"

"Yes I am."

"The program starts at three-thirty. If I gave you the number, would you be willing to call in some time after that?"

"Three-thirty? Sure thing."

The door burst open and slammed against the wall, revealing Jim Brenan framed in the doorway.

"Jim!" Martha said.

"Kendall! The cliffs are starting to collapse!"

"What?" Dr. Park stared. "Oh, uh, Dr. Faulkner, I need to go." He dropped the receiver.

"Just as I was leaving, the cliffs started to collapse!" Mr. Brenan motioned outside. The sound of his truck motor echoed through the Brenan's entryway.

"But the talk show!" Dr. Park pointed to the clock. "I can't miss it."

"We've got to get out there to help the other men!"

Dr. Park picked the phone back up and dialed Jonathan's

number. "Son, it looks like I'm not going to make it for the radio show."

There was a moment of stunned silence. "What?"

"The cliffs are collapsing at the graveyard. Jonathan, I've already made arrangements for several scientists to call in. It wouldn't be fair to cancel the show because of me. I want you to go ahead with our plan. Have your mom drive you and Jessie to the studio."

"But, Dad—"

"It will be okay, Sherman will be there. Son, just remember, Neal West is very smart. I would say as little as possible and let the scientists speak. I'll be praying for you."

Jonathan sighed, "I'll be praying for you too, Dad."

Dr. Park hung up and dashed for the door. "Okay, Jim, let's go!"

Jonathan rubbed the insides of his knees together. He was sitting in the studio with Mr. Bott and Neal West, the show's host. Mr. Bott looked uncomfortable. Mr. West, however, looked quite comfortable and overly confident. He wore a black sports coat and his hair was combed straight back from his forehead and cemented with gel. He was fussing with a stack of papers under the microphone, which hung from the ceiling.

A big digital clock hung over the exit door. Mr. West watched it intently as the final countdown approached. "Here we go. Three. Two. One." A bare bulb in the wall flashed red.

"Good afternoon from beautiful Santa Fe, New Mexico. You're listening to talk radio's best, *Chat Line America*! I'm Neal West, your host, heard for two hours from coast to coast. Well, those of you who tuned in last week will remember our guest Sherman Bott, the director of Genesis Foundations." Mr.

West waved his hand at Mr. Bott to cue him up. "Sherman, welcome back to the broadcast."

"Thanks, Neal," Mr. Bott said.

"Last week I challenged Sherman to try and find out the names of real scientists who believe in creation and then come back on the show." Mr. West turned toward Jonathan. "Now, folks, I wish you could see this—I have here in the studio with me a *boy*. No offense, but you look a little young to be a scientist."

Jonathan pursed his lips. "I'm eleven."

"Sherman, do you want to introduce your guest?"

"Yes, of course. With me is Jonathan Park," Mr. Bott said. "He's the son of a vertebrate paleontologist that I was going to bring with me today—but he couldn't make it."

Mr. West smiled patronizingly. "Now Jonathan, do you consider yourself an expert on creation science?"

Jonathan shrugged. "Pretty much—yeah." He moved closer to the microphone in response to Mr. West's hand motions. "Why don't you give me a try?"

Mr. West scanned the call-list. "Better yet, we've got a call from twelve-year-old Rusty. Rusty, welcome to the program."

"Hello? Am I on?"

Jonathan's leg-muscles tensed. He knew that voice.

"Um, I have a question for Jonathan," Rusty said. "You believe in God, right?"

"Yes." Jonathan nervously wrung his hands, waiting for the punch line. He knew that Rusty must have a trick planned.

"How could God have existed forever? Everything has a beginning and an end."

Mr. West laughed. "I like this kid."

"What a dirty trick," Jonathan muttered.

"I'm sorry, Jonathan, were you saying something? You need to speak up." Mr. West nodded smoothly toward the microphone.

Jonathan glared at his mic. *Nice one, Rusty.* He felt like a fool. "I don't know," he stammered. "The Bible just says that God has always existed."

"Jonathan, you don't have an answer for my question, do you?" Rusty chuckled.

Outside in the station's lobby, Mrs. Park and Jessie sat listening to the interview, which was piped through the speakers.

Jessie whispered to Mrs. Park over the droning voices. "Mrs. Park, Jonathan isn't doing very well, is he?"

Mrs. Park shook her head. "I'm afraid not. Jessie, I think his pride led him into a trap. I'm afraid this is the fall we've been warning him about."

Jessie twisted her fingers together. She wanted to do something. If Jonathan hadn't started out sounding so cocky, he would have had an easier time answering Rusty's question, or at least explaining why he wasn't the best person to do so. Now, he was being mocked on national radio.

Rusty's voice came over the speakers. "Well, Jonathan, I guess you don't know *everything* after all!" He laughed and hung up.

"Regardless, Rusty," Mr. West said, "you've made an excellent point, thanks for being on the show."

Jessie groaned. This was going to be a long two hours.

"Kendall, look! We're too late!"

Dr. Park and Mr. Brenan stared through the truck's dusty windshield. The dinosaur graveyard was completely covered by mounds of red stone. The cliff had collapsed.

Kendall flung his door open. "Was anyone hurt?" he called.

"No, sir, everyone is okay." Joe, the foreman, ran towards them. "There was nothing we could do. It just collapsed right in front of us. This debris would take a crew of our size years to remove."

Dr. Park raked his fingers through his hair. "Our dream— it's gone. Why?"

Mr. Brenan laughed bitterly. "I guess we can forget about an on-going fossil dig for the public."

"Why did the Lord allow this?"

Mr. Brenan sighed. "Well, partner, maybe it's to test our faith. I'm sure He has a plan, but I don't think we can do anything for now."

Dr. Park smacked his forehead. "No! I forgot about the talk show! I'll bet we can still make it for the last hour."

Back at the radio station, Neal West was enjoying himself. "Well, Sherman, you've been pretty quiet. Do you have anything to add?"

Mr. Bott cleared his throat. "Neal, you're making a huge mistake. When it comes to explaining the universe, we're in the same boat."

"You mean, Noah's Ark?" Mr. West laughed. "Really, what *do* you mean?"

"As creationists, we believe in an eternal God, but evolutionists have to believe in eternal matter. The Big Bang doesn't solve anything because it said that all the matter in the universe already existed. Either you have to believe that matter is eternal, or that God is. To be honest, when we see all of the design in the universe, it seems that the Creator made the matter—that is the most logical explanation."

Mr. West shuffled his papers. "Well, I disagree, but it's time for a break anyway. We'll be right back after this."

The red bulb on the wall turned off and Mr. West grabbed

a glass of water. The door opened.

"Dad!" Jonathan jumped up from his chair.

"Hi, Jonathan." Dr. Park stepped inside. "Hello, Mr. West, I apologize for being so late, but I had an emergency at our dig-site."

"Dr. Park?" Mr. West shook hands. "I was beginning to wonder if you existed. Thanks for coming."

Jonathan settled back in his chair. Things would be okay now that his dad was here. His dad could handle these questions.

Now that he could relax, Jonathan looked around the room, noticing things for the first time. The walls were decorated with framed awards and posters. Most of the photos were of Mr. West in his studio. There was something strange about the way he smiled. His lips were always shut. Jonathan looked at the talk show host as he gulped some more water, and realized that his front teeth were slanted, as if somebody had punched him in the mouth. Maybe that was why he was on radio and not television.

The break ended, and Mr. West blinked at his computer screen. "I see that another scientist is waiting on the phone. The question is, does he believe in the literal account of Genesis? Let's find out."

It was Dr. Otto Berg, one of the creation scientists that Dr. Park had lined up. Dr. Berg's work in the field of astrophysics began over fifty years ago.

Mr. West looked surprised. "You're kidding. You really worked for NASA?"

"Yes, I was an original employee."

Dr. Park winked at Jonathan. Mr. West was going to have a few more surprises.

The calls kept coming in. At 5:28, Mr. West answered his last call.

"Who is this?" Mr. West said.

"My name is Dr. John Morris, and I am a geology professor, and president of the Institute for Creation Research."

"And what is the Institute for Creation Research?"

"Neal, the Institute is a group of scientists, all of us with Ph.D.'s in various fields of science: geology, biology, physics, and science education. All of us are thoroughly trained in our fields and have been professors at major universities. Most importantly, we're all Bible-believing Christians who believe in the Word of God."

"Thanks for the call, Dr. Morris." Mr. West looked at the clock. "Well, I am Neal West and this has been another edition of *Chat Line America*. We are out of time for today, and what a day. Sherman, although I'm usually right, I must admit that you proved me wrong."

"And Neal," Mr. Bott said, "we've only heard from about twenty scientists today. I want to remind you that there are thousands more all around the world who claim the truth of creation."

"Including Dr. Kendall Park. Thanks for being on the program."

Jonathan's dad nodded. "It has been great!"

"And Jonathan, I think you've been my youngest guest ever. Thanks."

Jonathan was glad to get away from the fluffy microphone and stretch his legs, which were aching from sitting for the past two hours. Out in the lobby, Mrs. Park, Jessie, and Mr. Brenan formed a 'welcome back' committee.

"Kendall, that was great!" Mrs. Park hugged them both.

"Boy, did you see how many scientists called in?" Dr. Park grinned.

"Dr. Park, thank you so much," Mr. Bott said. He looked far more comfortable now that the show was over.

"Sherman, thank *you*. It was wonderful to see that there are so many others who have rejected evolution like myself. A couple days ago I said that I felt like the Lone Ranger, but now I feel like Tonto with a whole regiment of Lone Rangers. Most of the scientists who called in were better qualified than me to be on that show."

Jessie grinned at Jonathan. "How is the radio star?"

Jonathan grunted. "I sure learned a lesson. I needed it."

Dr. Park sighed. "You know, all I could think about during the whole program was losing the dinosaur graveyard."

"Dr. Park?" The *Chat Line America* producer was holding a phone. "I have someone who is looking for you."

"This must be my day for receiving calls at other people's places. Okay, I'll take it."

"He has been on the phone in there for a long time." Mrs. Park tried to peer through the frosted glass on the office door.

"Do you know who was on the phone?" Mr. Brenan asked.

The door opened and Dr. Park came out with a huge grin. "You'll never believe what happened!"

"Then you'd better tell us, partner," Mr. Brenan said. "What's going on?"

"That was Dave Phillips. He was calling to be on the show, but was too late. He's a creationist who is currently working on his Ph.D. in paleontology, and knows several creationists who have been on dinosaur excavations. I guess there is a group of people from around the nation who have been on several digs together."

The graveyard, Jonathan thought. It has to be something about the graveyard. "Can he help you, Dad?"

"When he heard about our dinosaur graveyard, he said he could have a huge team of diggers ready to help us in just a couple of weeks!"

Mr. Brenan held his hands up. "Kendall, you're kidding—

right?"

"He thought we'd have that graveyard uncovered in just a couple of months! Jim, we've got our dream back! We'll be able to open the dig site up to the public after all."

"And begin construction on the museum!" Mr. Brenan added.

Dr. Park removed his glasses and rubbed his sleeve over his eyes. "Jim, not only has God allowed us to have our dream, but now we've found others to help us live it!"

Jessie clapped her hands. "It's like we've become part of a huge team of friends reaching the world with the creation message!"

Jonathan grinned. He felt great. The show had turned out to be a huge success, God had taught him a much-needed lesson in humility, and now the dig-site would soon be back in operation. He took a big breath.

"We've got an awesome adventure ahead of us!"

Study Questions

Disaster at Brenan Bluff
(Answers are on page 161)

1. What scientist did Grandpa Benjamin say was most likely a Christian and offered this quote to confirm: "this most beautiful system of the sun, planets, and comets could only proceed from the counsel and dominion of an intelligent and powerful Being.'?

   _____

2. Name at least one of Isaac Newton's accomplishments as mentioned in the story?

   _____

   _____

3. What did Louis Pasteur invent?

   _____

   _____

4. What did some of Pasteur's important experiments prove?

   _____

   _____

5. Finish Pasteur's statement: "the more I study nature, the more _____

   _____

   _____."

6. Why did Mrs. Park quote Proverbs 16:18, "Pride goes before destruction, and a haughty spirit before a fall," to Jonathan?

   _____

   _____

7. Who was John Woodward and when did he live?

   _____

   _____

8. What did John Woodward believe?

   _____

   _____

   _____

   _____

9. Name one of the real-life scientists interviewed on the radio program.

   _____

   _____

10. What did Dr. John Baumgardner, scientist with the Los Alamos National Laboratory, create on a computer?

    _____

    _____

11. What inventor said, "I find it as difficult to understand a scientist who does not acknowledge the presence of a superior rationality behind the existence of the universe as it is to comprehend a theologian who would deny the advances of science"?

    _____

    _____

    _____

    _____

African Safari

A blue helicopter slowly descended to the African plain. The draft from the rotors leveled the thick savannah grass and the blew wispy bushes far away from the landing site. The skids sank into the shifty soil and the engine quieted. A man jumped from the driver's side and hurriedly attached a portable stairway below the cabin door.

A second man stomped down the stairs and growled at the surroundings.

"What I don't appreciate, Edward, is being dragged out from under air conditioned splendor, into this—this wilderness."

The passenger's voice was almost as sharp as his profile. His jaw made a ridge on each side of his face and poked out into an irrepressible chin. The only softening aspect was a slender mustache which shaded a pair of thin lips.

"Dr. Cassat, please. I don't want to spoil the surprise." Edward seemed undisturbed by his employer's sharp tones. He was obviously used to them. Both men spoke with English accents.

"All right," Dr. Cassat grumbled. "I've allowed the charade to go on *this* long. Just tell me one thing."

"Yes, sir?"

"Why must Africa be so hot?"

Edward coughed. "Well, we are near the Equator, sir."

"Be quiet. It was a rhetorical question. This heat I have no control over—yet. But you saw all those mangy beasts we flew over?"

The men were now trudging up a slight incline. Sweat-beads streaked down both men's faces.

"Yes, sir, they're called 'endangered species,'" Edward said.

"Pests, Edward, pests. Fouling up all that perfectly good real estate. I detest these wide open spaces. The jungle is what I like—an asphalt jungle."

When the two men reached the top of the incline, they turned to look at the vast plain behind them. It was covered in coarse brown grass, with clumps of spindly trees scattered here and there . Edward took a handkerchief from his pocket, folded it neatly in half, and dabbed at the sweat on his forehead.

"This so-called 'wide open space' is the Lake Turkana Wildlife Reserve," Edward explained. "All of this, as far as the eye can see. One hundred square miles dedicated to the preservation of vanishing African species—and you own it."

Dr. Cassat grunted. "Must you remind me? What's the going rate in Africa to bulldoze and pave over one hundred miles?"

Edward smiled. "May I remind you, sir, that this is tribal land you're leasing, and our local Kikuyu chief is firmly committed to its conservation. And that includes mineral rights."

Dr. Cassat looked at his man sharply. "Mineral rights, Edward? So, that's your game."

"Edward! Edward!" A husky man ran up the other side of the slope shouting Edward's name.

Dr. Cassat growled. "What's wrong with the fellow? Did

he swallow a bullhorn? Who is that?"

"His name is Kamoya," Edward said.

"Edward! Edward! Over here!" Kamoya called.

Dr. Cassat stalked down the incline. "Calm down, Kamoya. What's gotten you so excited?"

The dirt was pockmarked by shovels. Two yellow hazmat suits and a pile of equipment lay nearby. Kamoya was pointing at a pile of dirt. His wide grin exposed nearly every tooth in his mouth.

"Here, sir, look! It's beautiful! You see, Dr. Cassat?"

"A pile of dirt. Yes, charming. What is it, an endangered ant mound?"

Edward lifted a small box from the ground.

"What's that device?" Dr. Cassat demanded.

"It's a Geiger counter, sir. It measures radiation."

"I know what a Geiger counter does. Hand it over."

"Place it next to the dirt, sir."

Dr. Cassat unhooked an attachment from the box and held it near the dirt. The device began beeping and a coy smile slowly stretched across the rich man's face.

"Don't be shy, sir." Edward was grinning. "Closer."

The beeping grew louder and louder, until it blocked out all the other sounds of the African wilderness.

"By the sound," Dr. Cassat shouted, "I take it that this dirt is radioactive!" He pulled the box away and the beeping died down.

"Uranium-235," Edward said. "Top quality. Reactor and weapons grade. We happen to be standing near what appears to be an enormous deposit of it." He lowered his voice to a whisper. "It's worth millions."

Dr. Cassat stroked his mustache. "You're speaking my language, I must say."

"But we do have that problem with the Kikuyu chief."

"Ah, yes, mineral rights." Dr. Cassat pointed at Kamoya.

"Perhaps we could have Kamoya here talk to them."

Kamoya shook his head vigorously. "No, sir. The Kikuyu no trust Kamoya. They know me too well."

"Regardless, I have the will." Dr. Cassat folded his arms. "All I need to do now is find the way."

It was a lovely spring Saturday at Brenan Ranch, and full-scale picnic preparations were in progress. The Parks were over, and both families had driven to a quiet spot on the ranch where they set up a portable grill. The dads fired this up while the ladies spread a blanket on the grass and distributed plastic plates and utensils.

Jonathan sprawled on the blanket next to Ryan and smiled as he watched the dads grilling. They were bent over the charred racks as if they were performing surgery. When the operation was finally over, they had two plates of chicken legs and burgers and another plate of charred *something*. Jonathan couldn't quite tell what it was.

"Anything I can do?" Jonathan asked.

"No, I think we're ready to eat," Mrs. Park said.

Grandpa Benjamin asked the blessing. "Our Father in heaven, we ask that You would bless this glorious picnic lunch and the skilled hands of the ones who prepared it. We ask this in the name of Jesus, amen."

"All right, everybody," Mrs. Brenan said. "Dig in!"

Jonathan speared a chicken leg with his fork. The outer layer was a little burnt, but the inside was nearly perfect. He piled potato salad and chips onto the remaining section of his plate.

"Mom, can I have a cookie?" Ryan asked.

"I think you need a sandwich first."

"What a day for a picnic!" Dr. Park exclaimed. "Warm sun,

green grass, red cliffs, and delicious food."

"And ants," Jonathan said. He flicked at a small parade forming on the blanket's edge.

Dr. Park turned to Jessie. "So, I hear you're making a creation presentation for your homeschool group?"

Jessie nodded. "Ever since we got trapped in the cave I've really become excited about creation science."

"Well, now that we've found a dinosaur graveyard here on the ranch, you can tell the kids about the fossil evidence for a worldwide flood."

"Doesn't the fossil record tell the history of fossils since the very beginning of time?" Mrs. Brenan asked.

Dr. Park nodded. "Close. You see, evolutionists believe it's a record of billions of years of evolution. They say it tells about the order in which evolution happened. However, creationists say that most of the fossils came from Noah's Flood. The Bible says that all of the land-dwelling animals that weren't on the Ark were drowned. All of that water and mud from the flood would have made millions of fossils."

Mrs. Brenan frowned over her glass of lemonade. "So, if the fossil record is used by both evolutionists and creation scientists, how can we prove which one is right?"

Dr. Park reached for another burger. "If evolution were true, that would mean that millions of animals evolved into millions of other types of animals over millions of years." He pointed to a pair of birds that were chasing each other nearby. "If dinosaurs actually changed into birds, then there would have to be hundreds of thousands of part-dinosaur, part-bird animals as the change was happening. These changing animals are called 'transitional forms.' When they died, they should have left some fossil evidence."

"But there isn't any!" Jessie said.

"You're right—and that is a huge problem for evolution. Just think about it—there should be hundreds and hundreds of thousands of transitional fossils in the fossil record."

"So what does the fossil record really look like?" Jessie asked.

"That's the exciting part!" Dr. Park said. "We see fossils that match extinct animal groups, like the dinosaurs in our graveyard. We also see fossils for animals still alive today, like those birds, but we don't see in-between 'transitional forms.' And that is what we should expect to find if creation is true— because God said He made all of the animals distinct from the beginning."

"Thanks for steering me in the right direction for my report."

"Speaking of directions—" Dr. Park turned to Mr. Brenan. "Jim, can you reach into that bag and hand me those blueprints?"

Mr. Brenan looked at his greasy hands, then at the leather bag. "I'm going to get fried chicken all over them. Is that okay?"

Dr. Park laughed. "They're only copies."

He took the blueprints from Mr. Brenan and spread them out in the middle of the blanket. Jonathan squinted at the lines, trying to make sense of the building's outline. Whatever it was, it was big.

Dr. Park cleared his throat. "As you all know, Jim and I have been planning to open a creation museum, Hidden Cave, and our dinosaur graveyard to the public." He paused, letting the suspense build. "These here are the preliminary drawings for the main building."

Everyone gathered around eagerly. Jonathan was impressed at the plan's detail. It looked tangible—it was more than a dream.

"Have you found a good piece of land on the ranch to build on?" Mrs. Park asked.

Dr. Park motioned to Mr. Brenan. "Jim, will you do the honors?"

Mr. Brenan grinned. "Well—you're sitting on it!"

Jonathan nearly jumped. No wonder the dads had chosen this spot for the picnic.

"Hidden Cave is less than a hundred yards to the south," Mr. Brenan explained, "and Brenan Bluff, where we found our dinosaur graveyard, is right over there within easy walking distance."

"The idea," Dr. Park said, "is to have a continuous working dig as an exhibit, with our museum visitors joining in on the fun."

Mrs. Park grinned. "You're just trying to get someone else to do your digging for you."

Everyone laughed but Dr. Park. He looked at Mr. Brenan.

"I wish it were as easy as that. Unfortunately, we've hit a snag."

"It's money," Mr. Brenan said. "We're not going to take government money, and even if we were, they probably wouldn't give it for a creation museum. So we need private funding—but we've been having a really hard time getting people interested in giving money for a creation museum."

Dr. Park nodded. "Even if we do get funding, we'll probably have to scale back to a tenth of what we planned." He folded the blueprints. "If we're able to build at all."

Grandpa Benjamin spoke. "I'm sorry to hear that, Son. It sounds pretty grim, but remember, God is in control." He rubbed his chin with his index finger. "Philippians 4:6-7: 'Be anxious for nothing, but in everything by prayer and supplication, with thanksgiving, let your requests be made known to God; and the peace of God, which surpasses all understanding, will guard your hearts and minds through Christ Jesus.'"

"Thanks, Dad."

"Everything that happens in our lives happens because the Lord allows it. Why? To draw us closer to Him. To make us more like the Savior."

Jonathan reached for a third cookie. When he listened to Grandpa Benjamin, he knew where his dad got his personality and his easy-to-understand way of speaking.

"Just trust God," Grandpa Benjamin finished. "Sometimes He says 'yes,' sometimes He says 'no,' and sometimes He says 'wait.'"

When his grandfather stopped talking, Jonathan realized that something had been buzzing for awhile, and was growing quite loud. A mosquito attack? He looked up.

"A helicopter!"

The buzzing became a roar as a low-flying chopper approached. It looked like a four-seater and had thick blue stripes wrapping round the fuselage.

"I think it's going to land here!" Jonathan said.

Everyone scrambled to their feet. The helicopter hovered over them for a moment, then swung down toward a level spot.

"Everyone stay *away* from the blades!" Mr. Brenan shouted.

Mrs. Brenan grabbed Ryan and held him close. Jonathan was glad that he was old enough to stand by himself, but he also edged away from the chopper. The grass under the helicopter was blown flat until the skids grounded and the rotors finally slowed. Three men got out.

Dr. Park gasped. "Angela, look—isn't that Zach?"

"Wow. He got old!"

"You can't be twenty-two for ever."

"Who is Zach, Dad?" Katie asked.

Mrs. Park answered. "The one in the middle is Zach Benson, your father's old college roommate."

Jonathan remembered stories about Zach Benson, who was just a few days younger than his dad. The two had gone to college together, and both had graduated as vertebrate paleontologists in the same class. Since then, though, Dr. Benson hadn't been around very much. Jonathan had only seen pictures in an old photo album.

The man on Dr. Benson's left was dressed in a tailored black suit, and walked a step behind the other men. The third man wore wrinkled khakis, a Hawaiian shirt, and sunglasses. His face was lean.

"Zach! What are you doing here?" Dr. Park called.

Dr. Benson strode toward them with a big grin on his face. "It's a bit dramatic, I know, but wait until you find out why we're here! No, I'm afraid a handshake isn't going to cut it, Kendall."

He wrapped Dr. Park in a bear hug and almost lifted him off the ground. The man in the Hawaiian shirt grunted.

"Well, am I going to get any introductions?" Dr. Benson asked, after he had released Dr. Park and let him recover his breath.

"Angela, you know."

"Pretty as ever, you haven't changed."

Mrs. Park blushed. "Thanks, Zach."

"My daughter Katie, son Jonathan, and father Benjamin." Dr. Park pointed to each in turn. "And these are our friends, Jim and Martha Brenan, and their children, Jessie and Ryan."

"It's a pleasure to meet you all," Dr. Benson said. "Here with me is Dr. Cassat and his assistant, Edward."

Edward nodded. "A pleasure."

"Dr. Park, I'm a man of few words, so I'll get to them." Dr. Cassat's voice was harsh, but it sounded to Jonathan like this was his normal way of speaking. "You're a vertebrate paleontologist and I need you for a fossil recovery effort on my game reserve at Lake Turkana, in Kenya."

Jonathan blinked. *Africa? Wow!* The last time a stranger tracked them down and asked them to go somewhere, they ended up in Florida. That seemed pretty neat at the time, but Africa? That would be incredible.

Dr. Park stroked his chin. "This is rather sudden, Dr. Cassat. Could I ask what kind of fossil it is?"

Dr. Benson answered. "*Australopithecus afarensis.*"

"Really?" Dr. Park looked impressed.

"I don't know *that* one," Jonathan said.

"Jonathan, one of the most famous *Australopithecus afarensis* is Lucy. It's a partial female skeleton discovered by Donald Johanson in 1974, not too far from Lake Turkana."

Dr. Benson nodded. "Our Lucy came up near Tanapoi, at the southern end of the lake."

Jonathan remembered his dad going over that area's geography with him. It was in Africa's Great Rift Valley, where lots of primate fossils had been found. Evolutionists were using them to try to link man to his so-called 'ape ancestors.'

Dr. Cassat snapped his fingers impatiently. "So far we have found what—teeth? A partial jaw?"

"And a hamate, which of course is a wrist bone, and a hip joint." Dr. Benson looked enthusiastic. "It really is an exciting find."

"Excuse me for interrupting," Dr. Park said, "but Dr. Benson here is a very good vertebrate paleontologist. Why do you need me?"

Dr. Cassat growled. "You see, the chief of the Kikuyu—the indigenous tribe on the land—has the final say when it comes to these matters. He is one of you. They all are, actually."

"Vertebrate paleontologists?"

Dr. Benson smiled. "No, born-again Christians."

Dr. Cassat continued. "The only way he is going to let us continue the dig is if we include a scientist with a Christian creationist's worldview. Someone such as yourself. Dr. Benson recommended you, so here I am. Of course, you'll be well paid." He smiled, wryly.

Dr. Park hesitated. "I just don't like the idea of flying off to Africa on a whim and leaving my family and commitments behind."

"Is that all?" Dr. Cassat shrugged. "Then bring them. Your family—my treat."

"I don't know. Jim and I have an awful lot of work to do here."

Dr. Cassat turned to Mr. Brenan. "Ah, yes, you're his partner in that museum venture. Oh, don't look surprised, I know all about it. Very well, you can come too, and I'll pay you." He glanced at his watch. "I want you all to be happy. Because if you're happy, Dr. Park can turn his thoughts to the task at hand. Our Kikuyu chief is happy. And that makes Dr. Benson happy. And that makes *me* happy. I like happiness."

Jonathan didn't think he looked like a very happy man, but he didn't say anything. He wanted to go to Africa.

Park's and the Brenan's excused themselves and stepped a few yards away to discuss the opportunity in private. Dr. Casset put his hands in his pocket and whistled to himself.

"Dr. Cassat," Dr. Park said, "we feel that this may be the Lord's way of providing some of the funding for our museum. We'll do it!"

The air throbbed with drum-beats and strange animal noises. The ground was brown and dusty, with waist-high savannah grass on each side of the dirt road. There were no clouds, and the sun was intense.

Jonathan was jittery. *A real African village!* The Jeeps stopped in the middle of the village, where a crowd of dusky Kikuyu surrounded them.

"The Kikuyu tribe believes in a warm welcome," Edward said. He waved back. "A beautiful people with a beautiful culture. I hope you all are able to get to know them as I have."

"We will," Mrs. Brenan said. "We've decided to make this a teaching expedition for the children. The timing is perfect. My daughter was just preparing a report for her homeschool group about human fossils."

Everyone climbed out of the Jeeps and stretched their legs,

which was much needed after the bumpy ride from the airstrip.

Dr. Benson nodded approvingly at Jessie. "Studying fossils has been a life-long study for me. I'm glad to see such a young lady finding an interest in the subject."

Jessie grimaced a little at being called *such* a young lady, but responded cheerfully. "I like to learn new things, and I think fossils are neat."

Dr. Benson turned to Dr. Park. "Speaking of fossils, Kendall, I've wondered how you reconcile the ape-man fossils now that you're a Christian."

"Zach, I used to believe the evolutionary story, but now that I'm a Christian, I've been able to look at the facts from a different perspective."

Dr. Benson laughed. "I'll bet."

"Zach, think of all the fossils claimed to be in the human evolutionary line. They fall into two categories: either they're within the range for modern humans, or they have traits similar to apes or chimps. There haven't been any half-man fossils."

"What do you mean, Dad?" Jonathan asked.

"A good example of this is the Neanderthals. For the most part, the Neanderthal skulls we've found have had slightly bigger cranial capacity than the *average* person—but no different from some people alive today."

Jonathan nodded. Basically, his dad meant that Neanderthals had big heads, but no bigger than some people today.

"Although some evolutionists are claiming that Neanderthals were an evolutionary breakaway from human ancestry, many other scientists now agree that Neanderthals were fully human. We've even found evidence that Neanderthals made musical instruments, buried their dead, and had religious traditions just like modern humans. Yet, most of the public has seen pictures of the Neanderthal people as ape-like brutes."

Dr. Benson looked slightly uncomfortable, but said nothing.

"What about the others?" Jessie asked.

"Another great example is *Ramapithecus*. When people found a few teeth and a part of the jaw, artists drew pictures that looked half ape and half man. Later, some more fossils were found, and it became evident that *Ramapithecus* was almost identical to modern orangutans. And that's what often happens—when they find ape fossils they make them look more human-like, and when they find human fossils, they try to make them look more ape-like."

Dr. Benson frowned. "I agree with you that the media will often hype things up a bit, but I disagree with your total rejection of evolutionary interpretation."

"How interesting," Dr. Cassat said, sounding very uninterested. "Two men who started down the same path but have arrived at two totally different destinations. Well, shall we get you all settled in?"

By now, everybody was out of the Jeeps and standing in the middle of the village. From where he stood, Jonathan could count twenty-two houses. They all looked similar, each with a rectangular door and a thatched roof that overshot the walls. Jonathan was surprised to see most of the Kikuyu wearing T-shirts and cutoff jeans. They didn't look like the wild tribesmen he had imagined.

"Uh, Dr. Cassat," Mrs. Brenan said, "there are several men going through our things in the backs of the Jeeps."

Dr. Cassat waved his hand. "Not to worry, Mrs. Brenan. It's just more of the Kikuyu's five-star service. They should have you unpacked and settled into your huts in no time."

Another Jeep pulled up next to them and the driver waved to the rich man. "Dr. Cassat!"

Dr. Cassat scowled. "Well, I certainly am popular today. Yes, Kamoya, what is it?"

Kamoya leaned over and swung the passenger door open. "Sir, we're having a—problem—at site twelve. We need you, sir."

Dr. Cassat shrugged. "Ladies and gentlemen, children, unfortunately, duty calls. I'm confident you'll be able to entertain yourselves."

"Why don't you drop us off at the dig?" Dr. Benson said. "I'm sure Kendall and Jim would like to get a first look."

As the Jeep drove away, Jessie turned to her mom. "Mom, can we go exploring too?"

"Yeah!" Jonathan and Katie said.

Mrs. Brenan looked around. "I don't see any harm. What do you think, Angela?"

"I think it's okay. As long as you stay close."

Jessie hooted. Jonathan was a little less expressive, but just as excited. Who needs Indiana Jones when you can explore Africa for yourself?

Edward added a note of caution. "You have free reign here at the compound and the surrounding bush. The only place *off* limits is the northeast quadrant of the park. We have—sensitive research going on out there. If you do venture out, I do ask that you all exercise caution. There are many wild animals about. Some are quite dangerous."

Jonathan trudged through the waist-high grass with Jessie and Katie trailing closely behind. It was like walking through a *National Geographic* picture. The plain was mostly flat, though there were a few hills and depressions, as well as some clumps of trees.

Katie glanced over her shoulder. "Guys, I think we're getting too far away from the compound."

Jonathan shaded his eyes. They were rather far away.

Actually, the huts were little dots and the people were indistinguishable. He hadn't realized how far they had gone. He was about to suggest that they head back when Jessie interrupted.

"Wait a minute. Look at this." Jessie pointed to two parallel lines of beaten-down grass. "Tire tracks? What is a car doing way out here in the middle of nowhere? There aren't any roads."

The tracks were easy to follow through the grass, and it looked like they led into a ravine ahead, which was fringed with trees.

"Come on," Jonathan said. "Let's go check it out!"

Katie grabbed his arm. "Wait, guys, you remember what Edward said."

Jonathan pulled away and started for the ravine with Jessie.

"This is Africa, guys," Katie called after them. "You never know what could be hiding in a ravine. Jonathan—Jessie—don't!" She waited a moment, but they kept going. "Oh fine, wait for me."

The ravine's slopes were covered by trees and rocks. The tire tracks led straight down to the leveled base of the ravine. Jonathan wanted to explore, but Katie did have a point. Anything could be hiding on the slopes. *I'd better stay alert*, he thought.

The tracks led to some type of work site full of trash and equipment. There were a couple of temporary buildings, like storage sheds, but no dwellings.

"What is this doing way out here in the middle of nowhere?" Katie asked.

Jonathan rattled an empty can with his foot. "I don't think the Kikuyu use this place. I mean, look at all this modern equipment."

"Look at these." Katie pointed to a pile of yellow suits.

"Rain coats?" Jessie responded. "Does it even rain here?"

"Look, they have some kind of symbol on them." Jonathan leaned closer. Each suit was printed with a black circle from which three shapes, almost like propeller blades, radiated. "Doesn't that stand for radiation?"

Jessie gasped. "These aren't rain jackets—they're radiation suits!"

Jonathan was immediately suspicious. Why would a game reserve have radiation suits? They wouldn't stop a wild animal attack.

"Remember what Edward said?" Katie reminded. "Don't go into the northeast corner of the park. There was some kind of research going on there."

Suddenly, something roared in the bushes. Jessie screamed. Jonathan's chest tightened as he grabbed the girls and backed slowly toward the ravine's mouth. He'd heard that sound in the zoo many times—but this wasn't a zoo. There was a live, wild lion in the bushes.

"Right there!" Katie screamed. "A lion, a lion!"

A head and mane poked out of the bushes, followed by a chest, stomach, and pair of powerful hind legs.

Jonathan gulped. "Yeah, that's a lion." He tensed his muscles, waiting for the spring. It was his job to stop the lion long enough for the girls to get to safety.

But the lion didn't spring. And it didn't roar again. It lay down on its side and began growling. It looked like a huge house-cat purring in the sun.

"What is he *doing*?" Jonathan said.

"You want to go over to him and ask?" Katie's voice was high.

"He's just laying there," Jessie said. "If I didn't know better, I'd say he was—smiling."

"Well, why doesn't he eat us or something?" Katie shook her fist at the beast. "Get it over with, lion."

"You really don't have to taunt him, Katie." Jonathan tugged on the girls' shoulders. If they could back up without

disturbing the lion—

"Leo!"

Jonathan jumped. The voice was coming from behind them.

"Oh, Leo! You bad lion. Scaring these children like that." It was Edward, walking fearlessly toward the lion. "You ought to be ashamed of yourself. Go on. Go home!"

The lion slowly got up and whimpered. Only now did Jonathan notice the skin-colored collar around the lion's neck. It was half-buried in the bushy mane.

"Go home!" Edward repeated.

Leo whimpered again and padded back into the bushes, his shoulders drooped and his tail tucked between his legs.

Edward chuckled. "I'm sorry, children, I neglected to warn you about Leo. He is our resident—er, watch lion, you could say. We found Leo when he was a cub raised him as a village pet. As you can see, he's quite harmless. He's very protective of the Kikuyu children—even gone up against other animals to save a life. Unfortunately for you, he does enjoy a good practical joke."

"Well, Kendall, what do you think of our dig site?"

Dr. Park scanned the piles of dirt and tools and the dozens of workers. "It's—big."

Dr. Benson smiled. "Dr. Cassat has deep pockets, and his hands haven't gotten stuck yet. Something strike your fancy, Jim?"

Mr. Brenan looked puzzled. "Zach, how did they find the original fossils?"

"Actually, Dr. Cassat's assistant, Kamoya, spotted them."

"You mean, they were just laying in the dirt? Just like that?" Dr. Park raised his eyebrows. Fossils were usually like buried treasure, only more fragile.

"Just like that. But since then, we haven't found anything."

Mr. Brenan spoke. "So why did Dr. Cassat hire so many men for this excavation if there haven't been any indications of more fossils?"

Dr. Benson shrugged. "That's the million dollar question. After the initial find, nothing turned up. So now we're digging out the recovery site."

In the park's northeast quadrant, a group of men in yellow hazmat suits grunted and sang terse native chants as they dug in the dirt. Kamoya led Dr. Cassat toward the site.

"Well here we are, gallivanting all over East Africa. Kamoya, you're starting to remind me of Edward."

Kamoya's face was stolid. "It was Edward who asked that I bring you here. He has called the emergency."

Edward approached, his usually placid face twisted into a worried frown. "Thank you for coming so quickly, sir. There is something here you need to see right away."

Dr. Cassat growled. "I don't see anything wrong, Edward."

Edward pointed to a long low building on a little rise above the dig site. Moaning was coming from its windows.

"Dr. Cassat, sir, the workers—they're starting to get sick now. The exposure is causing radiation sickness. We have ten more men out just today."

"We've given them radiation suits. What more do they need?"

"It's not enough. They need proper equipment. Modern equipment to limit their exposure to this ore. Sir, lives are at stake."

Dr. Cassat folded his arms. "We don't have time to get

equipment, Edward, you know that. Our time is running out. Besides, it would make people ask questions. Curiosity kills more than cats." He leaned closer to Edward, his eyes narrow. "Developing a conscience at this late hour, are we, Edward?"

Edward straightened. "Sir, it brings me no pleasure to say this. In the past your business practices were—unethical. Certainly, immoral. But they've never been murderous—until now."

"Edward, there has never been so many millions at stake."

The two men locked eyes. They glared at each other for many seconds, their bodies motionless. Then, slowly, Edward turned away.

"You're not dismissed," his employer snapped. "Where are you going? Edward!"

"I don't know." His voice was unsteady. "I've never had a conscience before."

"If we tell the truth we lose the mine, the money, and I really do not relish the idea of spending the rest of my life rotting in some prison cell! You too, Edward! We continue as planned! Edward!"

Kamoya interrupted. "There is something else."

"There always is, Kamoya."

"The American children were out hiking and found one of our sites. It is not too hard to put two and two together. In my opinion, they pose a serious security risk to this operation."

Dr. Cassat sighed. "Then I guess you'll have to remedy that."

Kamoya grinned. "Yes, sir. Kamoya will take care of the children."

Jonathan, Jessie, and Katie were nearing the compound after their adventure in the ravine when Kamoya drove up in a Jeep.

"Hello, children!" he called, stopping the Jeep. "You look hot."

Jonathan wiped his forehead on his sleeve. "No kidding. And I thought New Mexico's summers were bad."

"Are you too hot for some adventure?" Kamoya asked.

Jessie perked immediately. "Adventure? Where?"

"I was just talking with your parents. Dr. Cassat has asked me to ask them if it was okay to take you to our new research site in the northeast corner of the park. Want to go check it out?"

"Did our parents say yes?" Katie asked.

"Of course! There is no danger with Kamoya nearby. What do you say?"

Jonathan looked at Katie. "Sounds good to me."

"Okay," Katie said. "As long as there aren't any more lions."

Kamoya grinned. "Hop in, children."

"This is the fossil, isn't it? The one that got us all the way to Africa?" Mr. Brenan pointed to a neat row of bones at the dig site.

"That's it," Dr. Benson said. "Our initial discovery here represents—oh, probably about fifteen percent of a complete skeleton."

"Is this the famous Lucy?" Mr. Brenan asked.

"Actually, no, Lucy was found a hundred miles to the north. But strangely enough, these fossils look identical to the Lucy fossils." Dr. Benson frowned. "It's really weird."

"Has she been named yet?" Dr. Park asked.

"Well—" Zach grinned sheepishly. "I was thinking of the name 'Ethel.'"

"Lucy and Ethel? As in, *I Love Lucy*?"

"Together again!"

Dr. Park laughed. "That's cute, Zach, really cute."

"Sorry to interrupt your American TV cultural

references," Mr. Brenan said, "but what can you assume about this creature from these partial fossils?"

"It's a hominid, an early ancestor to humans."

Dr. Park raised his hand. "I hope you don't mind if I disagree with you, Zach."

"Oh, I'm used to it. What's your story?"

"Think about it, Zach. You're assuming it's a hominid because you believe that hominids existed millions of years ago."

Dr. Benson nodded. "I will grant you that the evidence is somewhat circumstantial, but I believe that human beings evolved from lesser forms."

Dr. Park squatted next to the bones. "Look at the jawbone for a moment." He lifted it carefully and ran his finger around the edge. "This jaw is 'U' shaped. That's typical of gorillas." He set the bone down and pointed at the others. "And look at these toes. They're curved. So are the fingers here. What does that tell you?"

"That this hominid clearly spent much of its life in the trees, not on the ground. I grant you that. But this hip indicates an animal capable of walking upright like a human. That's really the key reason for describing this fossil as a human ancestor."

"I agree," Dr. Park said, "but I would add that they can walk *somewhat* upright. Not like humans. More hunched over, like this."

Dr. Park let his arms fall, rounded his shoulders, and shuffled around the fossils with his back bent forward. The diggers stopped their work and stared.

"Not everything has changed since college," Dr. Benson said.

Dr. Park straightened. "Oh. Right. Well, anyway, that's an idea of how they could walk. Pygmy chimps walk just like that. When I look at this skeleton, I see an extinct created ape-like animal. Not an evolved form."

"What's this one right here?" Mr. Brenan pointed to one of the fossils.

Dr. Park picked it up. "It's a hamate, a part of the wrist. You see this here? This is a hook that the tendons grab on to. It's much larger than a human's. That gives it much stronger hands." He set it back down. "This fossil supports my hypothesis as well, that this skeleton is from an extinct, predominately tree-dwelling primate."

Dr. Benson shook his head. "I think we can agree to disagree, Kendall. By the way, you appear to have a fan club."

"Hmm?"

The workers had stopped digging again and were watching Dr. Park eagerly. They probably expected another exhibition.

"Oh." Dr. Park grimaced. "Today's show is over. But back to the point—if evolution is right, then there should be thousands of non-disputable ape-man fossils in the fossil record. However, the truth of the matter is that evolution can only offer a very few, questionable, so-called ape-man fossils. To me that settles it—the fossil record can't support evolution."

"I have a different interpretation."

"Zach, remember what David Pilbeam said?"

Dr. Benson nodded. "We took that class together, remember?"

"Well, I didn't," Mr. Brenan said.

"David is a well-respected evolutionary paleo-anthropologist," Dr. Benson said. "He said that 'paleo-anthropology reveals more about how humans view themselves than it does about how humans came about.'"

Mr. Brenan looked at Dr. Park. "Translation?"

"He said that the study of fossils can sometimes be more about our beliefs than in finding out the truth about our beginnings."

A helicopter approached, heading for the landing pad. It was Dr. Cassat's big blue chopper.

"I suppose he's come to check on the site," Dr. Park said. "He's a strange man. He doesn't seem very keen on paleontology."

"No, I think money is more his area of expertise." Mr. Brenan shaded his eyes. "I see Edward and Dr. Cassat, but who are those uniformed men with them?"

"They're Kenyan State Police!" Dr. Benson said. "They're waving us over. Come on!"

Jonathan stuck his head out the window and let the breeze whip through his hair. They had been driving for a while, much longer than he had expected, but the landscape was so similar that it was hard to determine how far they had traveled. For all he could tell, they might have been driving in circles. But he wasn't worried. Life was good. A Jeep to ride in, an African country to explore, a big dinner back at the compound to look forward to—

Sput. Sput.

The engine seemed to be having trouble. Kamoya pressed the gas pedal, trying to rev the engine. Instead, it spluttered again, then died completely.

"What's wrong?" Jonathan asked.

"I don't know." Kamoya turned the key, but the starter simply clicked. He tapped the gas gauge. "I think we are out of gas. Yes, we are out of gas indeed."

"Out of gas?" Jessie said. "But we're out in the middle of nowhere. There can't be a gas station for miles."

"We have the radio," Katie said. "We should call for a tow truck or something."

Kamoya opened his door. "I don't think the radio is going to work. The battery is dead. Well, site number twelve is about five miles down this road. If I start now, I *could* be back in a couple of hours."

"And leave us out here all by ourselves?" Katie opened her

own door. "Are you crazy?"

Kamoya shut Katie's door. "Trust me, children, with all the wild animals about, you are much safer here in the Jeep."

Back at the fossil dig site, two tight-faced Kenyan policemen were explaining the situation to Dr. Park, Mr. Brenan, and Dr. Benson. Dr. Cassat's hands were handcuffed behind his back, and his mustache drooped.

"So," Mr. Brenan said, "you're telling us this whole fossil dig was a distraction to keep the Kikuyu from finding out about this ore-mining operation?"

It was Edward who had informed the police about Dr. Casset's plans. His face was sad, but settled. "The fossils were stolen from a legitimate dig at the northern end of Lake Turkana. Dr. Benson was brought out to verify the find. When the Kikuyu wanted a creation scientist, Dr. Benson recommended you, Dr. Park."

Dr. Park faced Dr. Cassat. "So bringing us all the way out to Africa was what—an elaborate deception?"

Dr. Cassat only glared back, but Edward answered. "We needed the Kikuyu away from the mine long enough to remove the ore. The Kikuyu wanted you. Dr. Cassat gave them what they wanted."

"And I would have gotten away with it," the rich man said. "This traitor ruined everything!"

Edward sighed. "Well, sir, it looks as if we'll both have plenty of time to discuss this—behind bars."

One of the dig site radios crackled. "Kendall! Kendall, are you there? Kendall!"

Dr. Park grabbed the transmitter. "Go ahead, Angela. Is something wrong?"

Mrs. Park's voice was shaking with panic.. "Jonathan, Katie, and Jessie are gone!"

"Gone?" Dr. Park said. "Where?"

"We don't know. One of the villagers said they saw them get in a Jeep with Kamoya and head for the northeast corner of the park. I didn't give Kamoya permission to do that. It's been a couple of hours and they haven't checked in."

Edward turned to his former employer. "What have you done with them?"

Dr. Cassat twined his fingers, the links on the handcuffs chain clinked together. "Oh, why, why me? If that fool has done anything—" he paused and pointed to the helicopter. "We'd best look for them with that. I don't need any more charges against me than I already have."

"Coats, boots, shovels, umbrellas—wait. Umbrellas?" Jonathan shrugged. "I guess Kamoya is an optimist." He tossed the umbrellas over his shoulder and kept digging through the rubbish in the back of the Jeep.

Katie poked her head out. "What are you doing back there?"

"I'm looking for something useful in this flea market. I don't think Kamoya cleans his Jeep very often."

Katie joined him. "I don't like this," she said. "Kamoya knows the area. He's smart. How could he just run out of gas?"

"Maybe—aha!" Jonathan spotted a dusty red jerrycan. "We *didn't* run out of gas." He lugged the can to the side of the Jeep, twisted the cap off the gas tank, and started pouring.

"We can't drive this," Jessie said, hanging through the window. "We're not old enough. We'll get a ticket."

"I know *that*," Jonathan said, "but if we start the motor it will charge the battery so we can use the radio."

Katie frowned. "Why didn't Kamoya think of that?"

"I don't know, but I'm having serious doubts about Kamoya. Anyway, once we contact help, we'll be out of here in no time."

Katie shaded her eyes with her hands and wandered to the other side of the Jeep.

"Hey, Jessie, look over there. Is that Leo?"

Jonathan couldn't see, because he was bent over the tank, but he heard Jessie take a sharp breath.

"If it is, he's brought company. Guys, you'd better get back in here."

Jonathan tilted the jerrycan higher and emptied the last few glugs. "That's done." He dropped the can and jumped on the running board to see over the roof. There, no more than forty yards away, was a pride of lions.

Jonathan gulped. "Eight, nine—eleven lions. This is *not* good, guys."

"They look hungry!" Katie said.

The lions formed a semicircle and walked forward slowly, their tails twitching. They looked like huge house-cats stalking a mouse. Only, this time, Jonathan was the mouse.

"We better get out of here," Jonathan said. "We're going to drive after all. Katie, get behind the wheel."

"Me? Why me?"

"Because you're the only one tall enough to reach the pedals!" Jonathan tiptoed around the hood, afraid that the lions would charge if he showed signs of running. He eased the passenger door open, climbed in, and quietly shut the door. Katie was in the driver's seat.

"Okay, Katie, the keys are in the ignition. Start her up and let's get out of here."

"This better not go on my driving record when I grow up."

Katie clicked the seat belt, gripped the top of the steering wheel with both hands, and slammed the gas pedal with her foot. Nothing happened. She pumped it up and down, but the car was silent. The lions were now thirty yards away.

"Katie, keys!" Jonathan grabbed the key and turned it in the ignition. The starter clicked. Nothing.

Jessie leaned forward from the back seat, her eyes wide. "Dad says that if you pump the accelerator before starting the car, it'll flood the engine."

Katie threw her hands up. "Now what?"

A lion charged the left side of the car.

"He probably wants to be first in line," Katie said, her voice trembling. She shook her fist at him. "No cuts, lion! If you're going to eat me, then wait your turn! A little order and respect, please. You got that?"

There was something strange around the lion's neck. Jonathan squinted. "Wait a minute, he has a collar. It's Leo!"

With a roar, Leo ran past the Jeep and sent the closest lion sprawling on its back. The others crouched in the grass and watched the fight. Roars punctured the air and clumps of fur flew from the two beasts, but the wild lion was no match for Leo's well-fed strength. It quickly rolled away from the fight and ran for cover with a big patch of fur missing from between its shoulder blades.

"Get 'em, Leo!" Katie screamed.

"Go, Leo, go!"

"I don't believe it!" Jonathan said. "He's doing it! He's chasing the others away!"

The lions darted from the scene and disappeared from sight, probably to look for an easier dinner somewhere else.

As the roars faded out, a humming noise above faded in. It was a helicopter.

The Parks, Brenans, and Zach Benson stood in a Kenyan

airport waiting for their boarding call. People from a dozen different nations were strolling the aisles, and occasionally, a belated passenger would dash toward his gate. A muffled buzz came from the snack court nearby.

"What a week," Mrs. Brenan said. "Praise the Lord the kids aren't hurt from yesterday's adventure."

"It will be good to be home," Mrs. Park agreed.

"Jessie," Jim said, "I'll bet you have some pretty interesting information for your presentation to the homeschool group."

Jessie grinned. "I've learned so much about human fossils! I'm so glad we came to Africa, even though it was really a hoax. There couldn't have been a better way to learn."

Dr. Benson's flight was first, but he lingered together at the Parks' and Brenans' gate, making the most of his last few minutes together.

Dr. Benson slapped Dr. Park on the back. "I feel like we're just starting to get reacquainted, and now I'm flying back to Chicago, and you to New Mexico."

"Zach, let's stay in touch."

"I wish you guys well with the creation museum." Dr. Benson shook his head. "I've got to admit, it would be interesting to see a fossil dig run by creation scientists."

"You should fly out and see it sometime," Mr. Brenan said. "We've found hundreds of *Coelophysis* fossils."

"Can I ask, why is a *creation* museum so important to you? There are plenty of good fossil museums."

Dr. Park answered thoughtfully. "We believe that it's important to teach people that there is a Creator. Think about it, Zach. If you believe in evolution, you have to believe that you're no more than molecules that came together by random chance. But *we* want to teach people that there is a loving God who made us and has given us meaning and purpose. Think of how that change in perspective can change a life."

Dr. Benson's left eye twitched. "I must admit, you're a

changed man."

"Zach, it's not me. The Bible says in 2 Corinthians 5:17: 'Therefore, if anyone is in Christ, he is a new creation; old things have passed away; behold, all things have become new.' Zach, Christ can change your heart, too."

Zach held up his hands. "Hold on, friend, I'm not ready for this yet."

"Well, when you are, I'm only a phone call away."

Jonathan raced toward the adults from the food court, his camera bag flapping against his hip.

"Jessie, you've got to get over here. There's an Egyptian Cobra loose in the snack bar! There's this big, scary looking guy trying to catch it."

"Oh, wow!"

"Hold on, guys, I'm coming too!" Katie called.

"Flight 1723 for Chicago is now boarding," a woman announced on the loudspeaker.

"Well, Zach, I guess this is goodbye." Dr. Park held out his hand.

Dr. Benson paused. He reached for something in his bag and stopped, his hand still inside.

"Kendall, I know you were counting on Dr. Cassat's funding to help you build your museum. It's a shame you're going back empty handed."

Dr. Park waved at the little group around them. "Take a look, Dr. Benson. You see this family? My friends? This is what really matters. If the Lord wants that museum built, He'll open the doors."

Dr. Benson smiled. "Here, take this." He took a package from his bag. "It's the proceeds from the sale of a small piece of ore from that uranium mine. The Kikuyu own the mine now, and they're going to develop it—without harming the workers or the environment. They wanted to reward us for putting a stop to Dr. Cassat. It's not a lot, and it won't last, but it'll get you started on that museum of yours back in New Mexico."

Dr. Park glanced down at the parcel. Could this be the Lord's provision? Could this be why they came to Africa?

"But, Zach," Dr. Park said, "your name is on this package too."

Dr. Benson shrugged. "Yeah, it is. Take it. It's a gift, I insist." He paused again. "You know, Kendall Park, you and your family, and your friends—you *almost* make me believe in God."

Dr. Park grinned. "And you, Zach Benson, confirm my belief in miracles."

Study Questions

African Safari
(Answers are on page 164)

1. What was Dr. Cassat really interested in digging up?

   _____

2. What Bible verse says, "Be anxious for nothing, but in everything by prayer and supplication, with thanksgiving, let your requests be made known to God; and the peace of God, which surpasses all understanding, will guard your hearts and minds through Christ Jesus." ?

   _____

3. Why did Grandpa Benjamin share Philippians 4:6 with Dr. Park?

   _____
   _____
   _____
   _____

4. What kind of fossil did Dr. Benson tell Dr. Park they were recovering? What is the name of one of the most famous

fossils of this kind?

_____

_____

5. How does Dr. Park answer Dr. Benson's question, "how do you reconcile the ape-man fossils?"

_____

_____

6. Name the two "false findings" of half-man and half-ape that Dr. Park mentioned.

_____

_____

7. What was the main reason Dr. Benson suggested that "Ethel" was a hominid?

_____

_____

What was Dr. Park's reply to Dr. Benson's reasoning?

_____

_____

_____

_____

Escape from Utopia

A man maneuvered the steep stairs in the stands behind home plate at a minor league baseball game in Santa Fe, New Mexico. He balanced a cup-carrier with three drinks in his right hand and carried three bags of popcorn in his left. It was a night game, and the bright lights that ringed the stadium dimmed the otherwise brilliant stars in the black dome above.

The man sank into an empty seat next to a woman and a young boy. "I've got enough to feed a truckload of firefighters," he said, handing the snacks out.

"It's so good to have you home, Myles." The woman wrapped her arm around his shoulders.

"Thanks for bringing us here, Dad," the boy said.

"Kirk, when I was your age, my parents took me to ballgames all the time."

The crowd cheered as the home team's biggest slugger walked to home plate. He swung his bat twice in slow-motion, then took his stance next to the plate and waited.

The ball came in fast and low, but the slugger dug for it and sent it hurtling toward the back fence. The crowd roared and the Morgans jumped to their feet, watching eagerly as the ball neared the boundary.

"It's going, it's going—gone!" the announcer said. "Home run! What an amazing hit for . . . What is *that*?"

Gasps hissed from the crowd.

"Dad, what is it?" Kirk said.

Something was rising in the sky behind the scoreboard. Something big. Something with flashing lights and a green glow.

The stadium was hushed. The *thing* climbed higher, and higher. The farther it got from the stadium lights, the brighter it appeared. A faint swooshing, and bell-tingling noise replaced the usual stadium buzz.

Myles grabbed his son's arm.

"I think—I think it's a UFO!"

Late the next night, the Park and Brenan families were driving south on Highway 285, a hundred and fifty miles south of Santa Fe, New Mexico. Both families were crammed into the Brenan's van along with all of their luggage. Dr. Park tuned into a local radio station, which was playing a special broadcast about an unusual sight at a ballpark the night before.

"The batter had just hit a home run," an eyewitness said. "We were all watching when we saw these bright lights, and something that looked like a UFO shooting across the sky!"

Mrs. Park quickly turned off the radio and shivered. "This is why I hate going to Roswell—especially at night."

Mr. Brenan laughed. "Everything's going to be just fine."

"Jim's right," Dr. Park said. "Besides, this trip is important. Now that we're going to open our own museum, we really need to see the Robert Goddard display at the Roswell museum. It should give us some great ideas."

"Speaking of this whole UFO thing, haven't people been looking for aliens for a long time?" Jessie asked.

Dr. Park nodded. "You could say that mankind has always wondered about the possibility. But the modern search for extra-terrestrials began in the fall of 1960, when a man named Frank Drake began 'listening' to the sky on a radio telescope."

"I've heard about that," Jonathan said. "It's called Serti, or something like that."

"Actually, it's SETI," Mr. Brenan said. "The Search for Extra-Terrestrial Intelligence."

Dr. Park nodded. "That project is now being carried on as Project Phoenix by non-governmental agencies."

Mr. Brenan changed to the left lane to pass a slow white van. There were few cars on the road this late—it was nearly 1:00 A.M.

"Dad," Katie said, "what are they looking for?"

"The people at Project Phoenix believe that if there's intelligent life out there, they probably have the ability to make radio or TV signals, like we do. They're listening for anything that sounds like an intelligent signal from space."

"The funny thing is, they haven't found anything yet," Mrs. Park said.

"That's right." Dr. Park twisted in his seat, trying to find more space to stick his legs. "It's been over forty years, and they haven't heard a single non-natural signal from any place other than Earth."

Mrs. Park grinned. "Anyone monitoring *Earth's* TV broadcasts would have a hard time receiving intelligent signals as well."

Through the window, Dr. Park saw the brilliant array of stars over the desert. They were magnificent tonight—a thousand shining pinpoints slashed onto a black canvas. Dr.

Park had always found astronomy fascinating. Before he was a Christian he loved to stand outside on a dark night and imagine alien worlds in other corners of the universe.

Katie interrupted Dr. Park's thoughts. "Wouldn't some people say that even if we haven't picked up radio signals, there's other proof for aliens?"

"They've looked for aliens in many other ways as well. It was in the 70s—" Dr. Park ticked numbers on his fingers. "1976, I think. NASA launched two probes which mapped the surface of Mars and searched for life. Ever since then, billions of dollars have been spent on the search for life throughout the galaxy."

"That's part of what they're trying to do with all the latest probes to Mars," Mrs. Park said.

"So, Jessie, to answer your original question—people do believe in aliens, but scientifically speaking, there hasn't been any confirmed evidence, not even a clue, for intelligent life except for here on Earth."

Mr. Brenan pointed to a sign. "Just a few miles from Roswell." He winked at the rear-view mirror. "Maybe we'll find something here."

"I have a funny feeling about this," Mrs. Brenan said.

Jessie waved her hand. "Mom, this is going to be great!"

"What, are you kidding?" Dr. Park slapped his armrest. "The Park and Brenan families on a road trip? What could possibly go wrong?"

Ka-lump. The van began vibrating, and the needle on the RPM gauge soared into the red zone. Mr. Brenan swung into the road's shoulder and turned off the engine. The van slowed, then gradually stopped.

"Honey, what's wrong?" Mrs. Brenan asked.

Mr. Brenan shook his head.

"It sounds like your transmission," Kendall said.

Mrs. Brenan groaned. "If we're going to keep taking these road trips, one of us is going to *have* to get a decent van."

Headlights beamed through the back windows. A car—actually, a van—was stopping behind them.

Dr. Park eyed it warily. "I wonder what this guy wants."

Mr. Brenan and Dr. Park climbed out of their seats and walked slowly toward the other van. A small cross protruded from the muddy ditch that paralleled the road; a flower wreath adorned its shoulders. Someone must have died in a car accident here.

"Are you guys okay?" the driver of the other van called. His shoes clicked on the pavement as he walked closer.

"I think it's our transmission," Mr. Brenan said. "Is there an auto shop nearby?"

"The closest one is in Roswell, about five miles down the road." The man glanced through the back windows of the Brenan's van. "Look, this is an awful time of night for your families to be stranded by the side of the road. I'm in charge of a retreat center just over that hill." He pointed to a hill slightly ahead of them. A road wound down the hill and intersected with the highway. "We could call a tow truck, and you and your families could be our guests tonight."

Mr. Brenan extended his hand. "Thanks for your generous offer, Mr. . . ."

"I'm sorry, my name's Andy."

Dr. Park also shook the stranger's hand. "I'm Dr. Kendall Park. I'm sure glad you came along when you did."

"Yes." Andy smiled. "I think it was meant to be."

The retreat center was dark when the Parks and Brenans arrived. The main building looked like a small conference center, and the sleeping-rooms were in two wings which jutted straight out from the main rectangle.

Andy first took the Parks and Brenans to two rooms in the right wing, then led Dr. Park and Mr. Brenan to the lobby, where he said he had the number of a tow truck driver.

"I know the driver personally," Andy said, unlocking the door. "He's probably the only one who would come out at this time of night. He'll tow it into town for you."

Andy flipped a switch next to the door and the overhead fluorescents flickered to life.

Dr. Park stared. Strings of little crystals hung from the ceiling, and bigger crystals dotted the floor in thick glass cases. Framed newspapers and brightly-colored murals covered the walls. The floor was black marble, flecked with white, star-like dots.

Dr. Park was instantly suspicious. Andy seemed nice, but Dr. Park didn't actually know anything about him. And this building did *not* look normal.

"What exactly is the purpose of this center?" Dr. Park asked.

Before Andy answered, a door in the left wall creaked open and a man of short stature appeared. He ran straight towards Andy, not even noticing Dr. Park and Mr. Brenan.

"Andromedus!" he called.

"Andromedus?" Mr Brenan said.

Andy nodded. "That's my full name, but I go by Andy."

"Andromedus, the chosen time has come!"

Andy frowned. "Orion, where are your manners?" He motioned at Dr. Park and Mr. Brenan. "These are two visitors from the outside."

When Andy said 'Orion,' Dr. Park thought that it was an Irish name, like O'Malley or O'Connell. But then he remembered that Orion was a constellation. And with Andy's full name being Andromedus . . . something was weird.

Orion held up his hand. "Universal peace to you."

Dr. Park blinked. "Uh, right back at you."

Orion grabbed Andy's arm and started leading him toward the door. "We're late," he said.

"Sorry, Dr. Park, Mr. Brenan, I've got to go to a—well, a meeting. The phone is right over there, and the driver's number is on the list on the wall. Just pull the door shut after you leave. Breakfast is at ten o'clock."

The door slammed behind the two men. Dr. Park and Mr. Brenan looked at each other with puzzled expressions.

"I wonder where they're going at two o'clock in the morning?" Mr. Brenan said.

Kendall slowly scanned the walls. At first, it looked like a room with an astronomy motif, since most of the pictures had stars, and planets, and space ships. Then he looked closer. Those space ships weren't like anything from NASA. Most of them glowed green, and one had little pointy things sitting in chairs inside a glass cockpit.

Dr. Park gritted his teeth. "Something is telling me that this isn't a nice little family camp."

Jonathan eased the heavy door open and tiptoed into the hallway. He wasn't sure if there were people staying in the other rooms, and he didn't want to wake anybody up. Dim light came from round globes embedded in the ceiling. There was a small window in the right wall, but it simply mirrored his face, showing his hair sticking up in a forest of tangles. He yawned.

Something moved at the end of the hallway.

Jonathan tensed. Who could it be? He slunk against the wall but something jabbed his back. He spun around to find a three foot by two foot picture-frame. Jonathan stared at the image, trying to make sense of it. At first, he thought it was abstract art, but then he realized that the artist had *meant* to draw a goggle-eyed, five-legged creature. Jonathan shivered.

Whatever was at the end of the hallway came closer.

"H-hello?" Jonathan said.

The other person gasped. "Jonathan?"

"Jessie! Whew." Jonathan smiled in relief. "What are you doing?"

Jessie came into the light. Her loose hair fell around her shoulders. She looked tired. "Ryan is using the restroom, so Mom said I could use the bathroom out here. What about you?"

"Katie's not feeling well, so Mom woke me up and asked me to get her a ginger ale from the vending machine." Jonathan pointed to the picture. "I hope there aren't any of *those* wandering around."

"This place gives me the creeps." Jessie paused. "Do you hear something?"

"The lights are buzzing?"

"No." Jessie cocked her head. "It's coming from this window."

Jonathan couldn't see through the glass because of the glare. He managed to crack the window a few inches and immediately the noise grew louder. A chilly wind raked through the tangles in his hair as he and Jessie peered out the window together.

Little dots of light moved in a huge circle on what looked like a field. Jonathan squinted. It looked like hundreds of people were walking around with candles.

Jonathan looked at Jessie. "What are all those people doing out in a field at two-thirty in the morning?"

Jessie backed away. "We'd better tell our moms."

"Yeah." Jonathan shut the window. "I think this trip is going to be interesting. See you at breakfast."

Breakfast was served in a little room off the lobby. The breakfast bar was pretty similar to a regular hotel's, with bacon strips, scrambled eggs, little plastic cups of yogurt, stale croissants, and a fruit bowl of seedless grapes and sliced pineapple. An older lady with inch-long earrings was taking orders for omelets.

The Parks and Brenans pulled three tables together and piled them high with plates, bowls, and cups of orange juice. The kids ate quickly and excused themselves to go outside. Dr. Park gave strict instructions to not go far from the building. He wasn't sure about this whole place, and he didn't want the kids wandering off into who knows what.

Mr. Brenan speared his last slab of bacon with his fork. "This food isn't half bad," he said.

Dr. Park washed a biscuit down with a gulp of orange juice. "You might say it's 'out of this world.'"

"You never know!" Mrs. Brenan said.

Mrs. Park winked. "I don't like the way my egg jiggles."

"It's alive!" Mr. Brenan said.

Dr. Park dug into his last yogurt cup and spooned out a delicious mouthful of the blueberry-banana mixture. It wasn't exactly gourmet, but in Dr. Park's mind, no continental breakfast was complete without at least one pre-packaged cup of yogurt.

Mrs. Brenan glanced at the lady behind the breakfast bar, then leaned closer. "I'm really concerned about what Jonathan and Jessie saw last night."

The others scooted their chairs closer to the table.

"What kind of a place do you think this is?" Mr. Brenan asked.

Dr. Park shook his head. "I don't know, but if one more person says 'universal peace to you,' I'm going to lose it."

Andy entered the breakfast room from the lobby. He was followed by Orion and a young woman, probably about twenty-five, with a pony tail. Andy smiled when he saw the Parks and Brenans.

"Do you mind if we join you?" Andy asked.

Kendall gestured to the empty seats.

"You remember Orion, and this is Ursula."

The man and woman raised their hands. "Universal peace to you."

Dr. Park tried to turn his scream into a coughing fit, and Mrs. Park played along by thumping his back. The newcomers sat down unfazed by Dr. Park's strange antics.

After several gulps of water, Kendall regained his composure. "Andy, in all the busyness of last night, I never had the chance to find out what this retreat center is all about."

"We're the Utopians," Orion answered monotonously.

"Utopians?"

Andy nodded. "It's an acronym for Universal Teachings Of Peaceful Interplanetary Alien Nations."

Mrs. Brenan's cup clattered against the table top and coffee splashed over the brim. "You're an alien cult?"

"We are not!" Ursula retorted.

Andy put a hand on Ursula's shoulder and spoke calmly. "Ursula, it is true that some from the outside view us that way. But really, we are seekers of the truth. We think it somewhat arrogant to believe that we are the only inhabitants in this universe." He handed Mrs. Brenan a napkin to blot up the coffee. "What about you? Do you seek knowledge from our universal brotherhood?"

Mr. Brenan grunted. "To be honest, I'm just trying to figure out things here on Earth."

Orion leaned forward, obviously eager to discuss their

beliefs. "We believe that the universe is teeming with life. With thousands of planets similar to planet Earth, the chances for evolution to produce life elsewhere are overwhelmingly high."

Dr. Park saw his first opportunity. "Actually, mathematically, the odds are completely *against* evolution," he said.

"You sound pretty confident."

Angela cleared her throat. "Dr. Park is a scientist."

Dr. Park shrugged. "Well, I have a Ph.D. in vertebrate paleontology, but I've studied quite a bit of astronomy, and my brother Nathan is a Ph.D. astronomer who works for NASA."

Orion rolled his eyes. "Uh-huh. A cover-up artist."

Andy motioned him to be silent. "Very interesting, Kendall." He rubbed the sides of his thumbs together. "As a scientist, how can you *not* believe in evolution?"

"As a Christian, the Bible is the basis for my belief. And, unlike what you here from the media, there are actually many scientific reasons not to believe in evolution."

"Really?" Andy held up a finger to pause Dr. Park and waved to the lady making the omelets. "Delphius, I'll take one with potatoes, broccoli, cheese, parsley, and a dash of cayenne." He turned back to Dr. Park. "You were saying?"

"If you want an example, think of how complex our bodies are. The human body is made up of building blocks known as amino acids that string together to form proteins. And these strings have to be in precisely the right order to sustain life."

Orion raised his eyebrows. "So?"

"Let's compare a chain of amino acids to people standing in a line. Let's say that we have eighteen people. Do you know how many possible ways they could line up?"

Orion shook his head.

"Believe it or not, eighteen people can be arranged in a line in more than six quadrillion, four hundred trillion different ways."

"I can't even imagine a number that high!" Mr. Brenan said.

"Now here's the amazing part. If those people could switch places in line once every minute it would take them over twelve billion years to stand in every possible order in line. Andy, how old do you say the universe is?"

Andy coughed. "I believe some scientists now say the universe began with a big bang about twelve billion years ago."

Dr. Park laughed. "I don't believe the universe is anywhere near that old, but even using your number—do you realize that eighteen people moving every minute through the entire course of evolutionary history wouldn't have time to stand in all the different line-orders that are possible?"

Andy shrugged. "What's your point?"

"It takes an average of four hundred amino acids to make up one protein in our body—they have to be in perfect order. Then it takes sixty thousand proteins to make up a single cell. Even worse, our body is made up of trillions of cells." Dr. Park leaned forward. "Andy, if random chance can't even line up eighteen people in all of the possible ways in twelve billion years, I certainly know that random evolution couldn't have made our super complex human bodies."

The conversation was interrupted when Delphius appeared at the table with Andy's steaming hot omelet and potatoes. It looked delicious. Tiny bits of green parsley garnished the mound of cheesy eggs and crispy potato slices. For a moment, Dr. Park wished he had ordered that instead of his yogurt cup.

"Andy, if evolution is impossible, there can't be other life forms out there that have evolved."

Orion tapped the table. "You're forgetting one very important point. There have been many UFO sightings recently in this area."

Dr. Park shrugged. "I don't know what people are seeing, but I doubt it's alien in nature."

The Utopians looked like they wanted to continue the conversation, but Jim steered them intoa less controversial topic.

"Andy, I called the auto shop before breakfast. They said my van just needs a new clutch, and that it would be done by noon. Is there any way that we could get a ride into Roswell?"

Andy pursed his lips at hummed. "I'd love to help, but unfortunately I can't today—it is the continuation of the Parley of Light."

"The 'Parley of Light?'" Mrs. Brenan said.

Ursula nodded. "It's an annual two day festival for the Utopians—a ritual celebration of our universal brotherhood. We rehearse our future meeting with the Cosmutons." She smiled. "You're welcome to join us."

"No offense, but, we'll pass," Dr. Park said.

Andy glanced outside. "Of course, that's your choice, but you may want to reconsider." He nodded at the windows. "As you can see, your kids seem to be getting along famously with mine."

There were very few trees on the property, and the grass was the brown, spindly kind that comes up when there isn't enough rain. After leaving the breakfast room, the Park and Brenan kids strolled to a basketball court they had seen from the cafeteria window. It was a concrete court, with only one worn hoop.

A boy, probably sixteen, was practicing his free throws. Four girls sat talking on a bench just off the concrete pad.

Jessie went straight for the girls. "Hi! I'm Jessie. This is my little brother Ryan, and my friends, Jonathan, and his sister Katie."

The girls grinned and stood up. The oldest was probably seventeen, with bracelets on both arms and a necklace that fell over her blouse. She was the one who spoke.

"My name is Venus, and this is Luna, Star, and Pleiades."

She pointed to the boy at the free throw line. "That's Apollo."

Apollo waved, tucked the ball under his arm, and jogged towards the group. "Universal peace!" he said.

Jonathan smirked. "I feel like we just met the whole Milky Way Galaxy."

Ryan looked at the other children with wide eyes. "You guys believe in aliens?"

"Of course," Venus said. "There are probably tons of other civilizations that have evolved out there. So, you don't believe?"

Jonathan hesitated. He'd never met anyone who actually believed in aliens.

Katie cleared her throat. "Well, I've always been told they don't exist, but I've never—"

Jonathan cut her off. "Like my dad always says, the idea of any life evolving is impossible."

"What if life evolved somewhere else, and then was brought to planet Earth?" Venus asked.

Jonathan shrugged. "You're just transferring the problem somewhere else."

"What?" Apollo tossed the basketball away and propped his right foot on the bench. Jonathan thought that he looked interested in what he had to say.

"Life is too complex," Jonathan said. "There's no way to explain it but by a Creator."

Venus looked confused. "I don't know. Maybe. But what if our creator was a cosmic brother?"

"So, who made him?"

She nodded. "I see your point."

Jonathan wondered if he should talk about God. They obviously didn't believe in God—at least, not the God of the Bible. He squared his shoulders. He knew he should always share his faith with unbelievers, and he was happy to do so, but that didn't stop him from feeling nervous.

"The Bible talks about the Creator who has always existed.

He's the One who planted life here on Earth, and He told us how. And, He made humans in His image."

That sparked lots of conversation, so much that Jonathan didn't realize how long they'd been talking until his parents and Mr. and Mrs. Brenan came out of the building.

"I see you're all getting along," Mrs. Brenan called. Her tone was unsettled.

"Mom, these are our new friends!" Jessie introduced the galaxy and somehow managed to get all of their names right.

Jonathan's dad shook hands with the new friends, then tapped Jonathan's shoulder. "We'd better get back to our rooms."

Katie frowned. "But we're just getting to know these guys! I'm not ready to go yet."

"Katie, we're *all* heading back to our rooms."

Katie hung her head. "Yes, sir."

By four o'clock that afternoon, Jonathan was getting tired of sitting in their room. His mom and Katie were laying on one of the beds, reading, and his dad was out looking for someone to take them into Roswell. He wandered to the desk and began rummaging through the drawers. A phone book? Not interesting. An old black comb with red hairs stuck to the bristles? Gross, and still not interesting. He found another book in the back and pulled it out.

"Don't reached for hotels have Bibles in their drawers?" Jonathan asked his mom.

"Most of them."

"Well, this place has their own kind of Bible." He held the book up. "It's called *Bollo: A Speculative Guide to Extra-Terrestrial Cultures*."

Dr. Park came in, shaking his head. "That was weird. All day long I've been trying to find a ride into town so we can get out of here, but no one will take us."

Someone knocked on the door. Mr. Brenan walked in.

"Anything?" Dr. Park asked.

"Nothing. I even met our tow truck driver this morning, and he said he couldn't give us a ride because he didn't want to be late to tonight's 'Parley of Light' celebration."

Mrs. Park groaned. "I feel like they're keeping us here for a reason."

"That does it." Dr. Park slapped his knee. "Pack your stuff—we're getting out of here!"

Jonathan blinked. The asphalt shimmered and grew sticky. The heat baking through Jonathan's shoes made him think about the hot tubs he occasionally soaked his feet in at hotels. He rolled his shoulders, trying to ease the pressure from the duffel bag's straps. At first, carrying the bag like a backpack with his arms through the straps sounded like a great idea. Now, not so much.

Mr. Brenan called everyone to a halt and set his suitcases down. He rubbed his red hands and nudged one of the suitcases with his foot. "What's in here?"

Mrs. Brenan shrugged. "You know—moon rocks, crystals, a phaser—just the essentials for around here."

Katie had been lagging in the rear, but she now caught up with them. Her lips were tight, so tight that she looked like she was pouting. "I don't see why we had to leave all of a sudden, anyway."

Jessie tossed her duffle bag into the air and caught it. "I think this is kind of an adventure!"

Jonathan glared at his own luggage. *I'd find it much more*

adventurous if my suitcase was as light as her's.

A car sped by in the left lane. Jonathan wondered what they thought of eight people walking with all of their luggage along the highway toward Roswell.

"Kendall, do you think we'll really be able to reach Roswell before dark?" Mrs. Park asked.

"Yes, Honey, we'll make it long before dark."

Crickets chirped six hours later. The asphalt was still warm, but it no longer shimmered. It was a dull black, faintly lit by the moon, and occasionally washed by the headlights of a passing car.

Mrs. Park sighed. "Kendall, we didn't make it to Roswell by dark."

"Look, everyone," Dr. Park said. "I'm sorry I dragged you all out here."

"It's okay, you were just doing your best to protect everyone." Mrs. Park looked to the others for encouragement. "Right, guys?"

The chorus was weak.

"Dad, isn't there *any* possibility there are real UFOs?" Katie asked.

Mrs. Brenan groaned. "You guys have been talking about that for the last two miles. Can't we play twenty questions, or something?"

"I think they're playing forty questions," Jonathan said.

Dr. Park considered his words for a minute before responding. "Katie, remember that UFO stands for 'Unidentified Flying Object.' Sometimes they're just that, something that hasn't been identified. I'm sure most of the cases are people seeing a natural phenomenon, or what they *want* to see. Sometimes, it's intentional trickery. Some people

97

have even speculated that there's spiritual deception going on."

"Speaking of aliens," Mrs. Park said, "have you guys noticed that all the pictures at the retreat looked the same?"

Mrs. Brenan laughed. "Like Casper the Friendly Ghost on one of those starvation diets."

Jonathan looked up at the sky, thinking about man's fascination with aliens. He could understand how someone without a biblical understanding could look at all those planets and stars and think there might be life. He noticed one star in particular. It was very bright, and it was moving across the sky.

"Look, a shooting star!" Jonathan said.

It grew larger, and brighter. It was coming toward them.

"That's no shooting star!"

The crickets' chirping faded under a swooshing, bell-tingling noise as the bright *thing* came closer.

"Dad, it's a UFO!" Katie yelled.

Jonathan dropped to the pavement and hugged his duffel bag to his chest. He was afraid to look up, but even more afraid to close his eyes. The sound buzzed in his ears like a hornet's nest, and the light grew brighter and brighter. Everyone, even his dad, was crouching on the ground, waiting.

For a moment, the asphalt glittered in a green glow, then the object whooshed overhead and sped away.

A bright light lit the road again, this time from a van coming toward the Parks and Brenans. It slowed, then stopped in the opposite shoulder. The driver's window rolled down and a man's head stuck out.

"What are you guys doing out here at this time of night?"

Dr. Park stood up. "We're trying to get into town." He sounded shaken.

"Can I give you a lift?"

"Please."

Jonathan's muscles were still shaking when he climbed into the back of the van. He squeezed into the right corner and pulled the chest strap on his seat belt as tight as he could. He felt a little less vulnerable inside the car. Although the mysterious light was gone, Jonathan still felt a little scared.

Up in the front seats, Dr. Park was thanking the driver again for the ride.

"My pleasure," the man said. He flicked his direction signal on and turned onto an exit ramp. "By the way, I'm Lucius. Universal peace to *you*, my brothers."

Andy sat in a ten by ten office deep inside the retreat center. The overhead light was dim, but still strong enough to reflect off the row of crystals adorning Andy's desk.

Andy heard two gentle knocks on the door followed by one loud knock.

"Come in, Orion," Andy called. "Have a seat."

Orion plopped into the chair on the other side of the desk. "Andromedus, our lease is running out. Unless we find a new retreat center, we won't have a place for our annual Parley of Light."

Andy slid one of the crystals out of line and stroked it with his index finger. His eyes were hid in shadow, but a slight smile clung to his lips.

"Orion, what do you think of our new outsiders?"

"You mean the Parks and Brenans?"

"Did you know that they own a very large piece of property in Abiquiu? They're trying to build some sort of religious center on the property—a museum, or something." Andy slid the crystal back into formation. "It would be the perfect place for our new retreat center."

"But they're not followers of the Utopian way. They were even caught trying to get away from here last night."

"I know. Fortunately, Lucius was coming back from town when he saw them alongside the road." Andy winked. "Unfortunately, he was in too big of a hurry to take them into town, so he had to bring them back here."

"But Andromedus, they would never give us their land!"

Andy shook his head. He leaned forward until the light conquered the shadows under his eyebrows and shone on his cold, piercing eyes. "My children tell me that Dr. Park's daughter, Katie, is already beginning to question her beliefs. Then to see a real UFO last night—she may begin to investigate the Utopian way. It's possible the others may follow."

Dr. Park groaned. "I can't believe we're back here in—in Utopia!"

Jonathan agreed. Last night, he had thought their problems were over when the van driver offered them a ride. Then he said he didn't have time to take them to Roswell—and, it turned out, he was a Utopian headed right back to where they had come from. It was déjà vu, only this time Jonathan had blisters on his feet.

The Parks and Brenans were crowded into the Parks' room, trying to figure a way out of this alien-lover's nest. No one would take them, there were no cars they were allowed to drive, and it was too far to walk.

Jonathan snapped his fingers. "Why don't we call a taxi?"

Dr. Park shook his head. "I tried, but there isn't any cellphone coverage. It turns out the only land line is the one we used to call the tow truck driver. For some reason the door is locked, and no one can find Andy to ask to let us in."

"They haven't *forced* us to stay here," Katie said. "And can't they believe what they want?" Jonathan thought about the countless UFO and alien questions she had asked over the past couple days. She seemed enthralled by the whole idea. He wondered. . . .

Dr. Park set his coffee cup down and leaned closer, looking Katie in the eyes. "Katie, we need to be thankful for the help the Utopians have given to us, and to treat them with respect because they're also made in God's image, but we don't have to agree with their beliefs."

Jessie nodded. "Especially because they don't believe in the Bible."

"They never *said* that," Katie said. "Dad, can't people believe in the Bible, and still believe in aliens?"

"They can, Katie, but remember, the main reason that people believe in aliens is because they believe in evolution."

"Yeah, but—what if God created people on other planets? The Bible doesn't say He didn't, does it?"

Dr. Park hesitated. "While the Bible doesn't say specifically that there aren't other people out there, there would be some serious problems if there were."

"Like what?" Mr. Brenan asked.

"One problem is when man rebelled against God. In Romans 8:22 the Bible says: 'For we know that the whole creation groans and labors with birth pangs together until now.' The Bible tells us that *all* of creation was cursed as a result of man's sin. If there are other people on other planets, were they cursed because of what *we* did on Earth?"

Katie half-shrugged. "I've never thought about that."

"That doesn't sound like a just and loving God to punish innocent beings for *our* sin. The only other possibility is that all alien civilizations sinned at exactly the same moment throughout the entire universe. But that seems pretty far-fetched."

"What about Jesus?" Mr. Brenan said. "The Bible says that He came to die for our sins. If there were all kinds of other worlds with other people, did Jesus have to go from planet to planet, dying for each one?"

Mrs. Park shook her head. "No, that can't be. Remember what it says in Hebrews 10:10? 'By that will we have been sanctified through the offering of the body of Jesus Christ once *for all*.' And in verse twelve it says: 'But this man, after he had offered *one sacrifice* for sins forever, sat down on the right hand of God.'" She put her hand on Katie's knee. "So if Christ died once, He couldn't have died other times for people on other planets."

Katie pulled her fingers until the joints popped. She definitely wasn't convinced, but it looked like she was having a hard time figuring out a good counter-argument. Her eyebrows raised. "So why did God make the universe so big, if there isn't anyone else living there?"

"Katie," Mrs. Park said, "I think God is the divine Artist who created this big universe simply because He likes to create—like a painter who hides things in his paintings he knows no one else will see. He does it simply for His own good pleasure."

Mrs. Brenan changed the subject. "For now, we better come up with a way to get out of this place."

Jessie bounced out of her chair. "While you plan, do you mind if we go outside?"

Jonathan almost wished they would say 'no.' His blisters were enjoying some rest and relaxation. But they didn't say 'no,' so Jessie dragged him out of his chair and led the way downstairs. Katie came with them, but Ryan stayed with his parents.

Outside, they saw Andy's kids on the path toward the main building. Venus waved.

"We were just on our way to get some soda. You guys want to come?"

"Sure!" Katie said.

Jonathan glanced sideways as they walked, trying to remember their names. He knew Venus, the older one, and

Apollo, the boy, but the other ones were a bit hazy.

Apollo grinned at him. "So, now that you've seen a *real* UFO, are you a believer?"

"Not really."

News must travel fast here, Jonathan thought. They hadn't said anything to people about seeing a UFO. Lucius must have said something.

"Did they seek to contact you?" one of the girls asked.

"Who?"

"The inhabitants of the UFO."

"Oh." Jonathan shook his head. "Not exactly. By the way, your name was—Moon?"

"Luna."

"Luna. Right, sorry."

The vending machine was in a little room right next to the front doors. The Utopians began inserting quarters and cranking out cans of soda.

"You know," Jonathan said, "ever since we came here, everyone has been talking about all of the inhabited planets. The only problem is that Earth is the only one that can support life."

"What do you mean?" Luna asked.

"Earth is special. It's designed perfectly for us to live here."

Jessie knelt to pick up a dropped quarter. "I heard that if we were just a tiny bit closer to the sun, we'd be fried. If we were any farther away, we'd freeze to death."

Apollo handed a drink to Jonathan.

"Thanks!" Jonathan punched the lid open with the cap and watched the carbon dioxide steam out of the can. "You've heard of ozone? That's another way that Earth is special. It's part of the atmosphere that protects us from the deadly rays of the sun, while letting in the ones we need."

Jessie nodded. "My dad was telling me that the amount of oxygen in our air is just right. If it were a little less, we wouldn't be able to breathe. If there was more, the entire Earth would burst into flames."

"And what about the water cycle?" Jonathan said.

Apollo raised his hand. "Okay, got it. You could also point out the balance of nature, and how plants and animals all work together to survive. But why couldn't there be other planets out there that also support life?"

Jonathan folded his arms. "Name one."

Apollo hesitated. "Um, I don't know the names of any."

"That's because we've never found any place else in the universe like our planet. That makes Earth unique, and I believe the Creator made it for us."

Jessie finished her soda and tossed the can into a recycling bin. "Jonathan, Katie, you guys want to do some exploring?"

Jonathan tapped the inside of his right foot against the bottom of the vending machine. Little sparks of pain tingled in his toes. He shrugged.

"Sure."

Katie shook her head. "You go ahead. I want to hang out with these guys."

"Didn't you get enough walking yesterday?" Jonathan asked. "My feet are plotting mutiny, and this retreat center property is about as big as the Grand Canyon."

Jessie waved him on. "I just want to see what's in that barn."

Jonathan sighed. He was usually game for an adventure, but right now he kept thinking about one of those foot whirlpools that spin cool water over your toes. Still, the barn *did* look interesting. It was dilapidated, with peeling red paint and a front wall that leaked spotty shafts of sunlight.

"I don't think they use this thing anymore," Jonathan said.

Jessie pointed to the dirt road a few yards ahead. "These tire tracks look pretty recent."

The last time Jonathan had seen fresh tire tracks going to a strange place was in Africa, and there, he had met a lion. There weren't many lions in New Mexico, but this *was* an alien cult. Who knew what they might find lurking in the shadows.

The door-latch was broken, so they went inside. Enough light flooded through the doorway to reveal a hay-covered floor with rusty machinery and some stacked hay bales along the far wall.

Jonathan whistled in short blasts.

"What are you doing?" Jessie asked.

"Scanning this alien structure for signs of life."

Jessie trudged through the hay, looking at the rusty machinery and broken-down crates.

"Hey, look at this." Jessie pointed to something in the corner, near the line of hay bales. "We've been farming my whole life, but I've never seen anything like *this* in the fields."

The object had a long nose, wheels, and two wings.

"That's a huge remote-controlled airplane!" Jonathan said.

It looked new and was covered in a shiny black paint, the kind that reflects light. A remote control lay on the closest wing. Jonathan picked it up. It had a retractable antenna, two toggle sticks, and a bunch of other controls. There was also a red button on the bottom that looked like it had been custom added.

"What's that for?" Jessie asked.

"Only one way to find out." Jonathan hit the button.

A swooshing, bell-tingling noise filled the barn. Jonathan nearly dropped the remote control. It was the sound of the UFO!

Something glowed green on the other side of the barn. The kids approached cautiously, not sure what to expect.

Around the corner of the hay bales was a big blobby *thing*, with lights glowing on and off like the rack on a police car and dozens of reflectors which turned the whole thing into a green-glowing mass.

Jessie reached out cautiously and touched the side. "It's papier-mâché!" She gulped. "We'd better get out of here. I don't think we're supposed to see this."

"This must be the UFO we saw."

"I knew it was a fake! But this is small compared to how it looked last night."

Jonathan shook his head. "It just looked bigger because it was against the sky." He walked around it, looking for wheels, or wings, but there weren't any. It was just a big cone, like a rocket. "I wonder how they make it fly."

"Come on, let's go." Jessie pointed to the door.

"In a minute. First, I want to figure this out."

Jessie grabbed his arm. "Jonathan, we need to leave *right* now."

"That's it!" Jonathan pointed to three heavy-duty straps on the bottom of the UFO. "I'll bet these attach to the remote-controlled airplane. It's light enough to work."

A car engine grumbled outside. Tires crunched the loose gravel, and two car doors opened.

Jonathan looked at Jessie. This was not good. The only way out was the doorway—where the people from the car were about to enter. Jonathan scanned the barn for anywhere to hide. The only hidden spot was behind the hay bales where the fake UFO was, but that was probably the first place anybody coming in would go. Jonathan looked at the stack of hay bales. There was a chance that the newcomers wouldn't look *up*.

Jonathan formed his hands into a scoop and boosted Jessie up, then clambered after her and crawled to the far end where the bales touched the barn wall. The rough stalks scratched his cheek as he lay flat on the top hay bale.

Voices grew louder. They were close.

"I thought we left this door closed," a man said. It was Andy.

"Wind must have blown it open," Orion said. "So, what time are we going to be at the Convention and Civic Center tonight?"

"Nine should be good. After the UFO flyby we'll still have time to get back for tonight's Parley of Light."

The Utopians were right next to the hay bales as they started wheeling the airplane toward the door.

"Andromedus, you're a genius. This UFO idea has really paid off."

"No kidding. In the last six months, our membership has doubled, our donations are up forty percent." Andy's voice rose. "It's like a UFO revival! Just think, Orion, we'll build our following until our re-uniting with the Cosmutans!"

"Remember, we still need a retreat site, and quick."

Andy chuckled. "My kids are working on Katie Park. If we can keep the families here, I think they'll see the Utopian way soon enough."

Jonathan clenched a fistful of hay. So that was their plan. Convince Katie of their lies, and then use her to convert the rest of them. Now that he knew about the fake UFO, he could stop the Utopians—but first he needed to get out of this barn.

More wheels squeaked outside.

"Here's the delivery truck."

Orion grunted as he picked up one end of the UFO. "This delivery truck idea is a winner—the truck drops off food and drives away with the UFO. No one the wiser. Good thing the driver is such a committed Utopian."

Another man entered the barn.

"Universal peace!" The man snickered. "You guys won't believe what just happened. I was stopped by the outsiders—they wanted a ride into town."

Andy grunted. He sounded preoccupied. "Helios, help Orion load the UFO. I'll bring the plane later. I'm going to set it just outside until I find the remote control . . . it seems to be missing." His voice snapped back to its usual tone. "What did you tell them, Helios?"

"I told them I had one more stop and then I was heading into town."

"Yes, well, I think you need to just 'forget' to pick them up. I'm not ready for them to leave yet. Besides, you need to get this UFO over to the Roswell Civic Center."

Jonathan clenched his hands tighter, thinking of the surprise he had in store. Then, it happened. The UFO flashed, and the bells began ringing. *Oh no!* He had been holding the remote control in his hand—he must have hit the red button.

"What the—" Andy spun around and looked up. "It's those kids!"

The three Utopians blocked the path to the door. There were no windows. There was only one other way out.

"Jessie, follow me!" Jonathan kicked the wall and smashed through a layer of rotten slats. It was a long jump. "Hold my hands!"

Jonathan grabbed Jessie's hands and lowered her as far as he could. She dropped to the dirt. THUD!

Andy was quickly clawing his way up the bales. Jonathan dug his feet into the hay and leveraged his back against the wall so that he could push. The bale shifted, then began toppling down on Andy. Jonathan didn't wait to see it land, but scrambled through the hole and jumped.

"Let's go!"

The kids ran toward the main retreat center. They had hardly passed the barn door when the three Utopians emerged.

"Load the UFO!" Andy yelled. "I'll get the kids."

Jonathan winced as each step squeezed his blisters. If Orion and Helios loaded the UFO and got away, Andy could deny its existence, and just say that he had an airplane for fun.

Andy's puffing was close behind.

Jonathan gasped. "Faster!"

They were approaching the main building. Surely Andy

would stop chasing them before people could see. *Right?*

"Jonathan! Jessie!"

Jonathan and Jessie pounded toward the corner of the building, around which their families had just turned.

Andy's footsteps slowed. "Please, stop! I can explain." His breath came in gasps.

Jonathan collapsed next to his dad. He still clutched the remote control in his right hand. "The UFO is a fake!"

"What?" Dr. Park looked down at Jonathan, then at Andy.

Andy walked up to them, his face red from running. He held out his hands as if to stop them from getting the wrong idea. "I think there's been a—a misunderstanding."

"In what way?" Dr. Park asked.

Jonathan planted his palms in the dirt, heaved, and scrambled to his feet. "The UFO we saw is in the back of the delivery truck."

Other Utopians began gathering around. Andy's children ran out to join them.

A motor noise was coming from the barn area. It was Helios. He was driving the delivery truck down the dusty road toward the group.

Jessie cupped her hands. "The UFO is a fake, and it's getting away in the back of that truck!"

Andy raised his hands. "It's not true." He tried to laugh. "I have no idea what these kids are talking about."

The truck was coming closer. If it got past them without stopping, there would be no proof. Jonathan gripped the remote.

"Here comes the air force." Jonathan pressed down the toggle stick. It was just like the R/C plane he had at home, only bigger. He pressed the switch for full power.

The plane hurtled toward them, quickly passing the delivery truck. Jonathan focused on the wings, tilting slightly to the left, then right, bringing it in a circle to face the speeding truck.

"What are you doing?" Jessie asked.

"Just a little game of chicken."

Jonathan hit full power again, and this time the plane was headed straight for the truck. Helios didn't have many options—if he drove straight, the plane would smash into his windshield. The truck swerved sharply to the right, and stalled in a ditch. The wheels spun loose dirt into the air, but the truck didn't move. It was stuck.

"Drive!" Andy yelled.

The engine revved, but it was no good.

Dr. Park ran toward the ditch. "Come on, everyone, I think it's time to take a look in the back of that truck."

The Utopians crowded around the back, waiting for the doors to open. Andy moved as if to block the door, then stopped, folded his arms, and hung his head. The doors swung open.

There was the fake UFO, just a mass of papier-mâché, lights, and reflectors. The Utopians gaped at Andy.

Venus touched Andy's arm. "Father, what's going on?"

Andy sighed. "We have a lot of talking to do."

The Parks and Brenans sat in the police station. Ursula was also there, since she had been the one to drive them into Roswell.

A policeman entered the room. "Dr. Park? Thanks for coming down here." He shook hands with Dr. Park and nodded pleasantly at the rest. "I've got to make a quick call, then I'll be right back. Please, take a seat."

"Ursula, thank you so much for driving us here," Mr. Brenan said.

Ursula nodded. "You're welcome, but please, call me Mary."

"Mary?"

Ursula—or Mary—sighed. "That's my real name. I've been Ursula for the past six months. It all started when I saw the UFO. I had questions, and I thought Androm—Andy had answers."

Katie cleared her throat. Jonathan watched her carefully. He wasn't sure how she had taken these recent revelations, especially when she found out that converting her had been one of the Utopians' main goals.

"Dad, I need to confess something." Katie looked at the floor. "Even though I believe the Bible, I didn't know how to explain what we saw."

"You mean the UFO?"

Katie nodded. "We saw it with our own eyes, and it seemed so real. It kind of shook me."

"I know what you mean," Mary said. "I fell for it too."

Dr. Park wrapped his arm around Katie's shoulders. "I think this has been a good lesson. Sometimes things look one way, when in reality, the truth is totally different. John 17:17 says: 'Sanctify them by Your truth. Your word is truth.'"

"We can always trust God's Word," Mrs. Park said. "He doesn't lie to us. As humans, we have the tendency to trust our own thinking more than God."

That sounded familiar to Jonathan. He raised his hand. "Isn't that what you say about evolution, Dad?"

"You're right. Science will say one thing and then change later to say just the opposite. That's what scientific theories are all about. It's about doing our best to describe how our world works, and then changing those theories once we find out more about it."

Mrs. Park put her hands on Jonathan's shoulders. "I guess the problem comes when we use man's scientific theories and observations to interpret the Bible, instead of just believing God's word. In the end, God will always be shown to be right."

"Just like our UFO," Dr. Park said. "You saw it with your own eyes, and it seemed real. But when you investigated it, it

JONATHAN PARK: A NEW BEGINNING

turned out to be fake. It's the same thing about believing where we came from. Many people want to believe in evolution, so they try to make it fit with the Bible. But when you look at the facts, science shows that evolution is wrong. It's too bad people believe in what they want to, instead of just trusting the Creator."

The policeman entered the room with a pen and notepad in his hand. He took a seat in the swivel chair behind the desk and poised his pen.

"Thanks for waiting. You said you're here to report a UFO fraud by a group called the 'Utopians?'"

"Yes!" Mr. Brenan said. "They held us captive."

The policeman tapped the paper with his pen. "Did they physically keep you from leaving?"

"Well, no, but they wouldn't give us a ride into town."

The policeman nodded sympathetically, but still didn't write anything down. "That's a shame, but unfortunately that isn't considered kidnapping by the law."

"What about the UFO fraud?" Dr. Park asked.

"I'm sad to say, it's just not against the law to fool people."

Mrs. Brenan looked shook her head. "They were tricking people into donating money and joining their little band of alien-wannabes."

The policeman dropped the empty pad onto the table. "I'm sorry. You might want to check with a consumer protection agency to see if they can do anything about it."

Dr. Park raised his hands in disbelief.

The policeman ignored the gesture. "What about you guys? Do you have a way to get home?"

"Yes, Mary here will drive us to a motel for the night, then we're picking up our repaired van in the morning and heading back to Santa Fe."

"Then you're free to go." The policeman extended his hand. "Thanks for stopping by. Drive safely, buckle up, and— universal peace to you."

112

Study Questions

Escape from Utopia
(Answers are on page 166)

1. What did Frank Drake do in 1960?

   _____

   _____

2. What does SETI stand for and what is the new name of the project?

   _____

   _____.

3. What example did Dr. Park use to show how random chance could not create the universe?

   _____

   _____

   _____

   _____

   _____

   _____

4. How did Jonathan answer the question, "What if life evolved somewhere else, and then was brought to planet Earth?" and "Who created the creator?"

    _____

    _____

    _____

    _____

    _____

    _____

5. What is the main problem of believing God created people on other planets? What does Romans 8:22 have to do with this?

    _____

    _____

    _____

    _____

    _____

    _____

6. How did Mrs. Park answer Katie's question, "So why did God make the universe so big, if there isn't anyone else living there?"

    _____

    _____

    _____

    _____

    _____

7.   Beside Earth, do we know of any other planets that could support life?

_____

_____

The Clue from Nineveh

Jonathan squirmed in his seat. Mr. Benefucio's science class was his favorite, but he always dreaded these report days when all the kids got up to spout about evolutionism. It was Rusty's turn, and he was talking about his frog.

Rusty held a plastic cage in one hand and tapped the walls with his other, making the frog leap back and forth.

"He was a tadpole when I caught him, but now he's got frog legs."

Rusty flicked the side again and the frog nearly flipped. Jonathan was sorry for the creature. Rusty would probably skin him alive or poke out his eyes after class.

Mr. Benefucio nodded. "Good, Rusty. Now, tell the class why you chose this for your biology project."

"Because you've been teaching about evolution."

Jonathan snorted. "That's not evolution."

Mr. Benefucio frowned. "Jonathan, this is Rusty's turn." He nodded for Rusty to go on.

"It is *too* evolution, isn't it, Mr. B.?"

The teacher stroked his chin. He was obviously thinking of a way to explain how it wasn't evolution while still teaching more about evolution.

"Rusty, I can understand why it would look that way, but actually—"

Jonathan raised his hand.

"Yes, Jonathan?"

"I can explain why it isn't evolution."

Rusty sneered. "Good for you."

"Take it easy, Rusty." Mr. Benefucio nodded at Jonathan. "Since you were polite enough to raise your hand this time, go ahead and explain to us why this isn't evolution."

"Because tadpoles turn into frogs all the time, but we don't see apes turning into people."

"That is correct. The DNA code of a tadpole already determines that it will become a frog, whereas in the case of apes, no single ape ever changed into a human during his lifetime. Instead, ape-like creatures were the ancestors of humans."

Thad Sherman, leader of the Eagle's Nest, raised his hand. "Not according to the Bible," he said.

Mr. Benefucio's smile stiffened. "We're not discussing the Bible. We're talking about science."

"My dad says science and the Bible go together," Jonathan said.

Eddie nodded. "My dad says that too!"

"And Eddie, he's entitled to that viewpoint. But this isn't Sunday School, and we aren't here to argue religion." Mr. Benefucio's voice softened to its usual tones. "Anyway, Rusty, what we see right now with your changing tadpole could be called growth, or even metamorphosis, but not evolution. Still, it's a fascinating process of nature."

As Rusty walked back to his seat, Jonathan raised his eyebrows at him.

"I told you."

Rusty stopped. "Yeah? Maybe you'd like to explain it to me after school." He leaned over Jonathan's desk, his fist clenched. "We'll see some real evolution, 'cause your nose is gonna turn into a blob of jelly."

"Sit down, Rusty!" Mr. Benefucio said.

Rusty gave one last fist-shake and stomped to his own seat. Jonathan fought the reflex to rub his nose. Rusty usually followed up on those kinds of promises.

Mr. Benefucio rapped his desk. "Who'd like to be next?"

Rusty raised his arm. "Why don't we let the *expert* go next?"

"That's fine with me," Jonathan said.

"Is it?" Mr. Benefucio nodded. "Maybe you should. It will give you a chance to use up some of that excess energy."

Jonathan lifted his two terrariums from under his desk and quickly checked to make sure his lizard was still in the green one. It was sleeping in a pile of grass.

"Instead of an amphibian, I picked a reptile. I brought my pet lizard."

"He probably thinks his lizard was a tadpole once," Rusty said.

Mr. Benefucio frowned Rusty into silence. "Thank you. Okay, Jonathan, I'm sure you enjoy having a pet, but the purpose of this assignment was to show us something interesting or unusual about nature."

Rusty spoke again, louder this time. "Lizards are *only* interesting to my cat. He eats them."

"Rusty, your next comment will send you to the principal's office, understood?"

Rusty nodded.

"Go ahead, Jonathan. What is it about this lizard that you find so interesting?"

Jonathan shrugged. He liked to act nonchalantly when he was about to surprise people.

"He's going to show us a miracle."

"Excuse me?"

"My lizard is going to prove that miracles happen."

School superintendent, Barry Brussell, dropped his cigarette stub into an ashtray and reentered the office building. His phone was ringing when he reached his desk.

"Yes, Ruth?"

A female voice responded. "Principal Lou Phipps from Painted Dunes Elementary is on line one."

"Thank you, Ruth." Mr. Brussell stared at the blinking keypad for a moment, then squared his shoulders and hit the button for line one. "Superintendent Brussell here. How can I help you?"

"Superintendent Brussell? My, that sounds so formal. Didn't your secretary tell you it was me?"

Mr. Brussell's goatee jerked as his jaw-bone flexed. "State your business, Mr. Phipps."

The other man laughed. "Now what kind of a greeting is that? You used to call me Lou. Aren't we on a first name basis anymore?"

"We never were on a first name basis."

"Not originally, no. But after I bailed you out of that little crisis and saved your job—I would say we got pretty chummy after that. Don't you agree?"

Mr. Brussell balled his fist. "I'm giving you the count of one to get to the point."

"Ouch!" Lou Phipps was still acting pleasantly. "Barry, you need to relax."

"That's all. I'm finished." Mr. Brussell held the phone away from his ear, ready to slam it down.

"Hang up the phone and you *will* be finished," Mr. Phipps said.

Mr. Brussell clenched his teeth and put the phone back to

his ear. "I knew it! I knew you'd never be satisfied."

"Just a little more hush money." Mr. Phipps was back to his pleasant, almost coaxing voice.

"You couldn't have spent it that fast!"

"You'd be surprised. There's mortgages, car payments, braces for my girls. You know what an orthodontist charges these days? Well, you remember what it was like *before* you figured out a way to get rich. Just share the wealth a little. No sense forgetting the little people who put you where you are. Time to be fair to your ol' pal Lou."

For a moment, Barry silently tapped the desk with his index finger. "Supposing I decide not to be fair?" he finally asked.

Mr. Phipps chuckled. "You don't want to disappoint me, Barry. What you want to do is meet me tonight and find out how you can get me out of your hair for good. How about coffee? My treat."

"I'm busy tonight. I've already made plans."

"Aw, change the plans, Barry. Be flexible for ol' Lou. Jenny's Restaurant. Six o'clock. We'll get an early start, so that way you'll still have the rest of the evening free for your lovely family. Jenny's. Got it?"

The phone clicked.

Back in the classroom, Mr. Benefucio was frowning at Jonathan.

"Are you mocking this assignment?" he asked.

"No, sir." Jonathan gulped. "Honest."

"Jonathan, this is a science class, and we know that miracles are a matter of faith."

"I'll prove it, Mr. Benefucio."

Rusty laughed. "Go ahead, Preacher Boy."

Mr. Benefucio turned on him. "You just used up your last chance. Head to the principal's office."

"But—"

"Nothing to discuss."

Rusty paused at the door and wrinkled his long nose at Jonathan. "Hey, Park! When I'm finished with you, they'll need a miracle to put you back together." He slammed the door behind him.

Mr. Benefucio sighed. "All right, Jonathan. I guess I'll just go along with this until we see your demonstration. But I warn you, your grade weighs in the balance."

Jonathan thanked him. "This isn't an ordinary lizard," he explained. "This is a chameleon."

"I see. Well, it's certainly a marvel of nature. Are you going to demonstrate for us how it changes color?"

"Yes, sir." Jonathan tapped the terrariums on his desk. "One of these is full of brown leaves, and one has green grass."

The terrariums were heavy, so the teacher had Thad carry one. Jonathan arranged them on Mr. Benefucio's desk so that the whole class could see the two habitats. He reached into the green one and carefully picked up his lizard, cupping the body in his hand so that the head and tail hung out.

"The lizard is green right now because he was in the grass terrarium. He has the ability to change color to match his surroundings. That way, he blends in and his predators can't find him."

"I wish I could do that," Eddie said. "It would come in handy during hide-and-seek."

Jonathan slid back the door on the brown terrarium and dropped the lizard inside.

"It'll take him a few minutes to change."

Mr. Benefucio nodded. "While he does, maybe you can explain why you call this a miracle. It's a fun thing to watch, and certainly an unusual phenomenon, but there *is* a scientific explanation, so it can't be called a miracle."

"Well, sir, I don't think there's really a scientific explanation."

Mr. Benefucio stared at him, probably trying to decide whether he was being defiant, or just ignorant.

"I just said that there *is* a scientific explanation, Jonathan, and as part of your assignment you are supposed to tell us what it is. You can't just bring a pet into class."

Jonathan stroked the brown terrarium. "I know the explanation, sir, but I think it only sort of explains it."

Mr. Benefucio folded his arms. "Tell us the explanation first, then we can discuss it."

Jonathan breathed deeply. He didn't mind public speaking, thankfully, but he wanted to be sure his logic was right.

"It's kind of like Rusty's tadpole. Just like the DNA code of a tadpole allows it to change into a frog, the DNA code of a chameleon gives it a special kind of skin pigment that allows color changes for the sake of survival."

"Well put, and very interesting, but hardly a miracle."

"Sir, I think it's a miracle because there is no explanation apart from God."

Mr. Benefucio frowned. "Always back to God with you. But you just *gave* us a good explanation."

"Well, we don't know how the DNA works. We know the lizard has it, and we know what it does, but we can't explain *why* the DNA programs it for protection. Not without God, we can't. A program needs a programmer."

"I know your beliefs about God, and you know *my* beliefs about bringing that up in science class."

Jonathan sighed. "Yes, sir."

"Hey!" Eddie jumped to his feet. "He did it! He turned brown!"

Lou Phipps hung the phone up and stared at the wall. He always put on a smooth act when talking to Superintendent Brussell, but his heart felt rotten. As long as he kept a tough outside, no one would know he was soft inside. Anyway, he was providing for his family. Isn't that what good dads do?

The door squeaked open enough to admit a head. Lou recognized the red hair and long nose immediately as Rusty's, his most frequent visitor.

Lou sighed. "What is it, Rusty?"

"Mr. Benefucio told me to come here."

Lou grunted. Biology. He'd probably let a snake loose in lab.

"Sit down, I'll be with you in a moment."

Lou hit the intercom button to his secretary's office. "Marge, call my wife and tell her that I need to meet with Superintendent Brussell tonight. I'll be home as soon as my meeting is over."

Lou swiveled to face Rusty. "What seems to be the trouble?"

Rusty stared at the desk, his wavy hair nearly blocking his eyes. "I dunno."

"You don't know? You must have done something."

Rusty looked at the carpet. "I didn't do nothin.'"

Lou leaned forward, his elbows on the desk, until Rusty raised his head high enough to look at him.

"Rusty, let me explain to you how this works. I ask you questions and you answer me. Otherwise, you'll be here on Saturday." Lou leaned back. "I have a pile of work to do on Saturday and I'd love to have some company."

Rusty shrugged. "I was talking, that's all."

"Must have been quite a conversation. What were you talking *about,* exactly?"

Rusty scowled. He was sitting up, now, looking straight at the principal.

"I don't remember."

"Oh, yes, memory." Lou flashed his best cold smile. "Tell you what. I've got a good book on refreshing the memory. I'll let you read it on Saturday. It'll help pass the time."

Rusty quailed. "Okay! Okay!"

"Ready to let me in on your little secret?"

"Yeah, all right."

"What a day!" Thad groaned.

Jonathan nodded. "I'm just glad it's over." He threaded the maze of chattering kids with Thad and Jessie tagging behind.

"Sounds like I missed a lot of excitement today," Jessie said.

"Just be thankful you're homeschooled." Jonathan wondered what it would be like to do school at home, without worrying about evolution, and God-haters, and Rusty.

Jessie kept talking. "I'm glad your dad has been doing so much work at the ranch. He's really nice to bring me back with him once in a while, especially when I need to use your school library."

Thad curled his fingers into his palm, like you would to hold a mug-handle, and coughed into his fist. "You may have picked a bad day to walk home with us, Jessie."

Jonathan whacked him with his backpack. "Come on, Thad! You're starting to sound like a scaredy cat."

"I'm warning you, buddy. You need to watch it. Rusty is twice your size."

"No he's not."

Thad frowned. "Fine, he's a hundred and fifty percent of your size."

Jonathan cocked his head, thinking of the percentages. *That sounds about right. Now, his muscles are probably twice my size.*

"I've seen him fight," Thad said. "It was more like a massacre."

And his feet are pretty big. I wonder if he kicks.

"Jonathan Park!" Jessie's shrill voice sliced Jonathan's thoughts. "Are you paying attention?"

Jonathan shrugged. "Rusty doesn't scare me."

"But he had to see Mr. Phipps on account of you," Thad said. "That might make him hate you even more. Mr. Phipps is mean!"

They had passed most of the kids and were approaching a small section at the edge of the yard that was nearly hedged off by bushes. A familiar voice sounded from inside the bushes.

"Leave me alone!" Eddie said. He ran out of the bushes, followed by Rusty.

"Get your hands off him!" Jonathan said.

"Hey, Park!" Rusty grinned. "We were just talking about you." He squeezed his right hand into a fist and punched his left palm a couple times.

Jonathan dropped his backpack. "Here I am." He tensed his stomach, trying to stop the knot-tying course inside.

Thad slipped next to Jonathan, his hands held out, palms forward. "Chill out, Rusty. Jessie's getting the yard duty teacher. You could get in trouble."

Rusty growled. "Oh, got your little friend to narc on me, huh?"

"I didn't tell her to call the teacher." Jonathan moved away from Thad. This was his fight, not Thad's.

Rusty raised his fists. "If you really believe in God, you'd better start praying, 'cause you're gonna need all the help you can get."

A whistle shrilled. "Stop that at once!" the yard duty teacher yelled.

Rusty smashed his fists together. "You're lucky. Another second—you'd have been tapioca pudding."

The teacher stalked between the boys and glared at Rusty. "You'd better come with me to the office."

"But I was just *at* the office."

"Then you should know the way. Let's get going."

Rusty looked back over his shoulder. "That means detention on Saturday. You're in big trouble, Park. All of you!"

Jonathan rubbed his forehead. It wasn't hot outside, but he was sweating.

"You look like you need a chocolate bar, or something," Eddie said.

"I'm all right."

Jessie shivered. "Let's get out of here before something else happens!"

Later that afternoon, Dr. Park was driving on the highway in his 4x4 truck when he received a phone call. It was Mr. Benefucio, Jonathan's science teacher. Apparently, Jonathan had participated in what the teacher called a 'disturbance' in class. Mr. Benefucio made it clear that 'religion' was not acceptable in his classroom.

"I'm sorry if my son created a problem," Dr. Park said. "I'm sure that whatever he said about God was from the heart. He has a passion for sharing the gospel."

"Believe me, I know." Mr. Benefucio sighed. "Look, Dr. Park, I'm not asking you to be hard on him, and I'm sure he has good intentions. If he could learn to talk about religion just a little bit less, our classes would run much more smoothly. That's all."

"Jonathan gets that from me, I'm afraid. It's nothing personal, but I do wish that our public schools would show both sides in the field of science."

"Both sides of what?" Mr. Benefucio's voice was still respectful, but it sounded as if he was restraining a laugh. "Dr. Park, I know you're a scientist. Surely you're not suggesting that I get up and read the book of Genesis out loud?"

Dr. Park grinned at himself in the rear view mirror. "Actually, I think that would be an excellent idea. The Bible is my standard for all things in life. That said, there is much objective data from paleontology and archeology which supports creation—things which are 'scientifically accepted.'"

"That, I'd like to see."

"I'd be happy to come in as a guest speaker any time you want."

"Wait a minute—you know I can't allow religion in the public school."

"I'm afraid I would have to disagree, Mr. Benefucio, as I have a different definition for religion than you, but I could present a talk about creation without even mentioning the Bible."

"How?"

"For starters, I'd establish that creation scientists actually point to observable facts when they make their arguments."

There was a long pause. "Dr. Park, if you can keep religion out of it—then you're on."

Jonathan galloped down the stairs two at a time. Without warning, Katie rounded the corner at the bottom of the stairs and blocked his path. Jonathan tried to spin away from her, tripped, and sprawled across the tile floor.

"Are you okay?" Katie asked.

Jonathan puffed air back into his chest. "Me? I'm fine. My knees?" He winced. "Not so much."

"Dad wants everybody in the living room." Katie helped him up.

"That's where I was going. What's it all about?"

Katie shrugged.

Jonathan's dad and mom and Grandpa Benjamin were already sitting on the couch.

"Is everything okay, Dad?" Jonathan asked.

"Mostly. Take a seat."

Jonathan settled onto the sofa next to Katie and waited. He tried to think of anything he had done wrong recently.

Dr. Park rubbed his knees. "Jonathan, I got a call from your teacher today."

Jonathan gulped. "Why?"

"He liked your experiment, but he didn't like your talking about God."

"Oh. Is he mad?"

"No, not exactly mad, but he doesn't want it to happen again."

Grandpa Benjamin grinned. "Even so, God has used Jonathan's words to give you this opportunity, Kendall."

Jonathan raised an eyebrow.

"I've arranged with Mr. Benefucio," Dr. Park said. "I'm going to teach your class about creation next week."

"But I thought he didn't want to hear about God anymore?"

"He doesn't, and I've agreed to restrain myself to only giving evidence for creation not included in the Bible."

"I have a feeling the Bible will still come up," Mrs. Park said.

"It may. Skeptics generally bring up the Bible themselves

when creation is discussed."

"Speaking of the Bible—" Grandpa Benjamin touched his chin with his index finger. That meant a Bible verse was coming. "Romans 8:28 says: 'And we know that all things work together for good to those who love God, to those who are the called according to *His* purpose.' Jonathan's presentation was used by God to bring Kendall into the class."

All things for good? Jonathan had a vision of red hair and a long nose.

"Grandpa, are all things going to work together with that bully who's picking on every one?"

Mrs. Park cleared her throat. "I believe you've been making that situation worse."

Dr. Park held up his hand. "Wait a minute. I don't approve of fighting as a general rule, but if Jonathan was merely defending himself—"

"Kendall, Jonathan was egging Rusty on in class."

Dr. Park looked sober. "Were you, Son?"

"I . . . guess."

"That isn't like you, Jonathan."

"But Dad, if you could just meet this Rusty. . . ."

"I know you think of this kid as the enemy, but has it occurred to you that Rusty may just be lonely? This is his first year at a new school."

Jonathan tried to picture Rusty as lonely. It wasn't easy to visualize.

"Maybe if he were nicer, he'd make friends easier."

"Jonathan, you're the Christian. You're the one to set the example. Do you remember the verse we looked at in family devotions last week?"

Jonathan sighed. He knew where this was going. "'But I say to you, love your enemies, bless those who curse you, do good to those who hate you, and pray for those who spitefully use you and persecute you.' Matthew 5:44."

Mrs. Park nodded. "You've certainly memorized it, but the hard part is learning to apply it."

"It *is* hard, Mom, but there are other parts of the Bible that are easier to obey. I don't mind the part about loving people—most people, that is."

Grandpa Benjamin leaned forward and touched Jonathan's knee. "It's easy to love someone lovable. But God tells us to love our enemies because Jesus wants us to forgive our enemies."

Dr. Park nodded. "Rusty probably isn't learning about God at home. You and your friends may be the only Christian witness he has."

"Remember, Jonathan," Mrs. Park said, "Rusty thinks you're his enemy and is every bit as bothered by the things you've said and done."

"But—"

"Don't tell me he started it, because it doesn't matter. Sin is sin. Jesus has forgiven your sins. Wouldn't you like to help Rusty see his need for a savior?" Jonathan's mom looked into his eyes. "Promise you'll be nicer to him."

She was right. Jonathan nodded slowly. "I'll try, Mom." He tried to smile. "But Rusty is so mad at me, I just hope I don't get hurt being nice."

Jonathan tried to sit perfectly straight with his back pressed against his chair like a ramrod. He grinned at his dad. Not only was Dr. Park teaching, but he was doing an excellent job. Even Jonathan, who had heard all the information before, was fascinated by the presentation.

Dr. Park looked at his watch. "I think now is a good time to review. Somebody explain to me, let's see, microevolution."

Elizabeth raised her hand. She was always attentive, the

best student in the class.

"Microevolution means 'small evolution.' Like if colored rabbits were seen by wolves in the snow more easily than white rabbits, after a while, only the white rabbits would survive and their children would be white."

"Exactly. That's microevolution, or what we all know as adaptation. Animal groups can change to adapt to their surrounding environment." Dr. Park pointed to Thad. "Thad, can you explain macroevolution?"

Thad straightened. "Uh, 'big evolution,' meaning that new animals come from—from—" he stopped.

"Macroevolution means that one kind of animal changed into another. Like dinosaurs changing into birds—but we've never seen that happen. Microevolution is completely different from macroevolution. Microevolution is proven by science— we see animals adapt and change for their environment, but no one has actually seen macroevolution, or one animal changing into another."

Mr. Benefucio was sitting at his desk, while Dr. Park stood in front of the blackboard, which was covered with the drawings that Dr. Park had sketched during his talk. Jonathan thought that the teacher seemed twitchy, but he hadn't stopped Dr. Park yet.

"Here's another problem for evolution," Dr. Park said. "Where did life come from in the first place? Evolutionists say that a bunch of chemicals came together by random chance, and then what?"

Eddie raised his hand. "Then those chemicals made molecules and all the plants and animals and everything go back to those original molecules."

"Exactly, but that's the problem. Science tells us that life has to come from life. Now kids, in science, nothing is considered proven unless it is observable. Do we observe any evolution today?"

"Yes!" Rusty said. Because Rusty sat in the seat closest to

the door, Jonathan couldn't see his face, but he was pretty sure that the bully had been watching him during the whole class.

"We do," Dr. Park agreed. "And what kind? Do we ever see one kind of animal turn into another? No, we don't. We see microevolution. We see different kinds of dogs, and different kinds of cats, but we don't see a dog evolve into a cat. We don't see life evolve from non-life. You see, evolution from one species to another has never been proven."

Elizabeth raised her hand. "You're saying our science book is wrong?"

Mr. Benefucio stood up quickly. "I'll answer that, Elizabeth. I don't happen to agree with Dr. Park, but I thought it would be fun to hear an alternative viewpoint today. You may choose to believe whichever theory makes more sense to you." He smiled. "Just make sure that on your test, you answer according to what I taught."

Elizabeth wasn't finished. "Maybe we don't see macroevolution, but we didn't see God make the world, either."

Dr. Park nodded. "That's true."

"And we don't see God at all, so God can't be proven."

The rest of the class murmured. Elizabeth's logic had obviously made an impression.

Dr. Park still looked confident. "Science *does* give us evidence for God. Most of what we call 'facts' in life are brought to us on the basis of evidence, not personal experience. For example—how many of you have ever been to Australia?"

Jonathan's classmates looked at each other, but no one raised a hand. Frank, two seats over, always liked to talk about his summers in England, but Australia was all the way on the other side of the globe.

"None of you?" Dr. Park said. "Then here is a question. Does Australia exist?"

"Yes!" Elizabeth said.

"How do you know? You haven't seen it."

Thad raised his hand. "Other people have been there."

"How do you know they aren't lying and making the whole thing up?"

Elizabeth laughed. "Everybody knows about Australia. It's in books, and pictures."

"And movies," Eddie said. "I watched a foodumentary about this weird Australian food paste called Vegemite, and they had all sorts of footage from Australia."

Dr. Park smiled. "What if the pictures are from some other place people just *called* Australia? And you didn't personally see the filmmakers filming. Are you catching on? None of you can prove that Australia exists, but then again, the evidence for Australia's existence is so enormous and obvious, that we accept it."

"But we have no eyewitnesses who saw God create the earth," Mr. Benefucio said.

"We have the witness of nature itself."

"How is that?"

Dr. Park pointed to the far back corner. "Rusty, I hear you did a report on a tadpole. Isn't it incredible that the genetic code of a frog existed in there ahead of time? Isn't it amazing that living creatures have something inside of them that can adapt and survive? Every design must have a designer."

"Yes, and that designer is nature," Mr. Benefucio said. "Dr. Park, you're obviously very knowledgeable, and I respect that, but there are too many stories in the Bible that scientists cannot take seriously."

"Such as?"

The teacher shrugged. "The very first one. Surely, you're not going to defend the story of Adam and Eve living immortally in the Garden of Eden and talking to a snake?"

A loud snicker came from behind Jonathan. It was a Rusty snicker.

Dr. Park remained unfazed. "Most definitely. And, there's

evidence from archeology."

Mr. Benefucio chuckled. "Really now? I'd love to hear about this 'evidence,' but we're out of time today." He looked at the class. "I think you really made a hit, Dr. Park. Maybe we can persuade you to come back sometime."

Many of the children applauded.

"I can do better than that," Dr. Park said. He gathered his notes into his briefcase and snapped it shut. "There's a finding from the ancient civilization of Ninevah which offers evidence for the biblical account of creation. This artifact has been in the British Museum for years, and presently is being toured in America." He turned to the class. "Kids, how would you like to take a field trip to our own Santa Fe Museum of Ancient Art to see a special clue from Ninevah?"

Jonathan led the class in a loud cheer.

"Mr. Benefucio?"

Mr. Benefucio tapped his fingers together. "Well—maybe—we'll see."

The desk-phone rang in Lou Phipps' office.

"Not another parent." Lou groaned. He picked up the receiver. "Lou Phipps here."

"Just what's going on at your school, ol' pal Lou?" Superintendent Brussell sounded angry, almost afraid. "I've spoken with two parents today."

Mr. Phipps opened his eyes wide. "Really? I've spoken with four."

"One dad was absolutely livid. Said he wouldn't stand for his daughter being exposed to religious ideas. He threatened the entire school district with a lawsuit!"

Mr. Phipps shook his head. "People act like the Gestapo is

going to take over the country if the word 'God' is mentioned in the classroom. It all seems rather harmless to me."

"And how harmless will it be if the school district gets sued?"

Mr. Phipps nodded. So that was the real impetus for the call. He pinched the receiver between his shoulder and neck and leaned back.

"Worried that if the plaintiff takes too careful of a look, they'll find out about your sloppy bookkeeping?"

Barry's voice lowered. "Look, you fool, if they find out about me, you can be sure they'll find out about who helped me cover it up."

Mr. Phipp's smile stiffened. He sat up straight. "Well, Barry, now *you* sound like the blackmailer. I didn't know you had it in you."

"I had a good teacher."

The intercom buzzed.

"Mr. Benefucio is here, sir," the secretary said.

"Send him in." Lou punched the intercom button off. "The culprit just arrived," he told Mr. Brussel.

"What?"

"Never mind. I'll take care of this. Nothing to worry about." Lou hung up. So, Mr. Benefucio was here. Well, Mr. Benefucio had some things coming.

The teacher looked nervous as he sat down. People usually looked nervous when they came to his office, Lou thought.

"How has your week been so far?" Mr. Phipps asked.

"It's been okay." Mr. Benefucio twitched a smile. "And yours?"

"About as well as a principal's week ever goes, I suppose. Mr. Benefucio, I understand there's been a lot of excitement in your classroom lately."

The teacher fumbled his fingers. "I always try to make my classes exciting, sir."

"Yes, I'm sure the kids appreciate it. What most interests

me, though, is the little circus you brought into town last Tuesday."

"It was hardly a circus, Mr. Phipps. He's a Ph.D.—a vertebrate paleontologist."

"I don't remember approving any paleontologist, vertebrate or otherwise."

"But—I've brought in guests before. So have a lot of other teachers. And just last week Mrs. Gardner had a mime speak to her drama class—well, I guess he didn't actually speak, but he performed."

Mr. Phipps slapped the desk. He wanted to make sure that his point was very, very clear.

"I don't care about some mime who pretends to climb a wall! If you ever bring religion into a classroom again, you better just be ready to transfer into the ministry."

"Sir, if you'll permit me to—"

"That will be all, Mr. Benefucio."

"But if I could just—"

"I said that will be *all*, Mr. Benefucio."

After school the next day, Jonathan went looking for his dad to ask him some questions about his new report assignment and found him talking on the phone in his room. Dr. Park gestured that Jonathan could stay.

"Are you sure you won't get in trouble for this, Mr. Benefucio?" Dr. Park asked.

Jonathan wondered why his teacher was on the phone. He tried to think of anything he had done wrong in class, but couldn't.

The phone was in speaker mode, so Mr. Benefucio's voice came through clearly. "This is a voluntary trip, not on school time, so what can Principal Phipps do?"

"A lot. Take it from one who's been in a similar situation. But I do admire your courage."

Mr. Benefucio grunted. "I don't buy into this creation stuff, but your point about letting the kids hear both sides has been nagging me."

"Well, I'll call Mr. Ash, the museum curator, to tell him the trip is on. See you on Saturday!" Dr. Park closed the cellphone. "Good news, Son!"

"I heard! Can I invite Jessie?"

"Of course. Then our whole family should spend some time in prayer. Your teacher is taking quite a risk."

That Saturday, Lou Phipps entered his office late. He liked to sleep in on Saturdays. Really, he'd like the whole day off, but his workload just wouldn't allow for it.

The message button was flashing red on his phone, but before he could even grab a notepad to start taking them down, the phone rang.

"Lou Phipps here."

A shrill voice blared in his ear. He held the receiver a foot away and blinked as a steady stream of words piped through the phone line. The best he could make out, Mr. Benefucio's class was on a field trip to the Museum of Ancient Art with the creationist who had caused such a ruckus earlier in the week.

After about three minutes, Mr. Phipps took advantage of a brief pause. "Mrs. Lassater, please, as a parent, I understand your concerns—"

"You said it wouldn't happen again, Mr. Phipps!"

Mr. Phipps held the phone away until he was sure she had finished her sentence, then cautiously brought it back to his ear.

"I did not approve a field trip. Mr. Benefucio has done this entirely apart from my knowledge. It's Saturday. School isn't even in session."

"Well maybe we need a principal who knows what's going on at his school! They're there *right* now."

Mr. Phipps gritted his teeth. What a way to start a day. "Mrs. Lassater, your son didn't go with them, so no harm has been done."

"Of course my son didn't go with them! I wouldn't let him, and now he feels left out."

"I promise to get to the bottom of this."

The phone clicked.

"Mrs. Lassater? Mrs. Lassater?" Mr. Phipps hit the intercom. "Marge, get me directions to the Museum of Ancient Art. Fast!"

"Yes, sir. Also, Rusty Mitchell is here to see you."

Mr. Phipps slapped his forehead. He had forgotten about ordering Saturday detention for Rusty.

"Very well, send him in."

Rusty slouched inside.

"Good morning, Rusty! I hear you're missing out on a little field trip today."

Rusty shrugged. "I didn't even want to go."

"Well, it seems we're both going."

"Huh?"

Mr. Phipps grabbed his keys and pointed to the door. "I can't leave you here. You're my responsibility for the day. Let's move it, Rusty."

Rusty slouched into his seat and stared out the window, away from Mr. Phipps. He obviously wasn't enthralled by the chance to spend a day with the principal.

"Rusty?" Mr. Phipps said.

"Yeah?"

"Doesn't your conscience ever bother you? Don't you ever feel bad, picking on people who are smaller than you?"

Rusty continued to stare out the other window. "I don't care. Survival of the fittest."

"I was a new kid at school once. I know how lonely it can be."

"I don't care."

"Sure you care. If you didn't care, you wouldn't get mad enough to hurt others. But Rusty, when you do that to others, you hurt yourself even more."

Rusty was silent.

"Rusty, look at me."

Rusty's face was hard, and his eyes were glazed, as if he had put up a mental shield. Lou remembered his own days as a schoolkid long ago. He knew what it was like to be inside that glazed look, and he felt sorry for Rusty.

"It's a bad thing to ignore your conscience," Mr. Phipps said. "If you ignore it too long, it will harden." Lou waited for a response, but nothing came. "You don't know what I'm talking about, do you?"

Mr. Phipps made his second to last turn and settled down for the last few miles before the museum.

"Rusty, let me tell you a story. It's about a boy your age who belonged to a club that his friends had started." It was Mr. Phipp's turn to look away. He could sense that Rusty was watching him, but without curiosity. "One day, just by accident, this boy found out that the club president had been keeping some of the membership dues for himself, after they were collected. The club treasurer, he was in on it too. He helped the president cover his tracks by doctoring up the club's account books. But, anyway, this other kid, he finds out about it, see?"

"What did he do when he found out?"

"At first he was going to rat on him to the others, but he didn't want to be a tattletale, so he did something even worse. He made the president pay him money to keep quiet."

"Really? Wow!" Rusty said.

"But he wasn't proud of himself. His conscience bothered

him a lot."

"Then why didn't he just give the money back?"

Lou nodded bitterly. "Sounds easy, doesn't it? It might have been, if he'd done it right away. But he got scared. He got scared because now he was in on the secret, and now he was just every bit as guilty."

Lou dug his thumbnails into the steering wheel.

"It started out as greed and it turned into fear. Then, because he was afraid to do the right thing he had to lie to himself and *pretend* he was doing the right thing. It was easy to justify himself because of all of the expenses and needs of his family."

"His family?"

"Well—not his family, his—just try to get the point I'm making. Do you understand? Sometimes people lie, even to themselves, because otherwise their conscience would be too painful."

"Is this a true story, Mr. Phipps?" Rusty asked.

"Yeah. It's true."

"Somehow I get the feeling this story wasn't really about kids in a club. It's something with you, huh?"

Mr. Phipps pulled into the museum parking lot. "That's not important."

"Did they ever get caught?"

Mr. Phipps stopped in a parking space. "No." He pulled the key from the ignition. "Not yet."

Inside the museum, Dr. Park was standing in front of a display in the room dedicated to traveling exhibits. Mr. Benefucio's science class was gathered in a semicircle facing him. There were several other borrowed artifacts from the British Museum displayed around the walls, but the main exhibit was right here where Dr. Park stood.

"Okay, come close so that everyone can see."

"What is it?" one of the kids asked.

"This is a greenstone cylinder from the Mesopotamia area." Kendall pointed at the details on the cylinder, his index finger hovering just over the glass. "The carving you see is called a 'seal.' Seals depicted stories and events in the ancient world. It was their way of recording history. Pay close attention to what's drawn on the seal, because that's why we're here."

The kids shuffled closer, the shorter ones craning their necks to look.

"Now, who wants to describe it for us?" Dr. Park asked.

A dozen hands raised.

"You." Dr. Park pointed to the closest girl. "What's that in the center?"

"A tree."

"And, what's sitting to the right of the tree?" He pointed to another child.

"A man!"

"And to the left? Eddie?"

"A woman," Eddie said. "She's plucking fruit from the tree."

"And what's that standing behind the woman?"

"It looks like a snake."

"But he's standing up," Jessie said.

"Yes he is, Jessie. When we read Genesis, we see God cursing the snake for tempting Eve. Part of that curse was that snakes now wiggle around on the ground. But they weren't like that before."

Jonathan raised his hand. "Is this a picture of the Garden of Eden story?"

"Yes, or more correctly put, this is archeological evidence that it's more than just a story."

Mr. Benefucio folded his arms. "Why do you say that, Dr. Park?"

"If the Bible is really true, then all nations and people descended from Adam and Eve. The history of these events would be handed down by each nation. Some of the details might have changed, as each culture exaggerated and perverted the exact retelling, but the basic story would remain the same. And that's the exciting thing about this stone. It's dated between 2200 and 2100 B.C., possibly around the time of Abraham of the Bible. While the Old Testament tells the story of Eden, this seal came from another people group and tells the same basic story!"

"Is this the only evidence?"

"Of course not. This is just what's on display in the museum today." Dr. Park looked around for his briefcase. "There's other evidence, such as the Sumerian account of the land of Dilmun. I brought a copy of that, a translation—but I think I accidentally left it in my car."

"Want me to get it for you, Dad?" Jonathan asked.

"If you don't mind." Dr. Park tossed Jonathan the keys. "It's in the trunk."

Thad raised his hand. "Can I go with him, Mr. Benefucio?"

Mr. Benefucio shook his head. "I want the class to stay together, Thad. Jonathan, you can take your guest, Jessie, with you if you want."

As Jonathan and Jessie walked away, Dr. Park turned back to the class. "While we're waiting, I'll tell you in my own words about this Sumerian account. It describes Dilmun as a land of perfection, a place where lions and wolves didn't kill, a place where there is no pain or disease or evil at all. . . ."

Lou Phipps and Rusty clattered down a museum hallway. "Help me look, Rusty." Mr. Phipps led the way, moving

JONATHAN PARK: A NEW BEGINNING

quickly. He wasn't going to let Benefucio get away with going behind his back.

"Hey, Mr. Phipps, I think I just saw Jonathan Park going toward those stairs with his friends." Rusty pointed to a flight of steps in a small hallway to the left.

Mr. Phipps frowned. "The lady at the front counter said Benefucio's class was down at the end of *this* hall."

"Can I just check real quick?" Rusty edged toward the hallway. "The class might have moved."

"Make it snappy. I'll keep heading down the hall. Meet me there in two minutes sharp, understood?"

Rusty pounded up the stairs to the second floor. Two glass doors led to an open-air walkway that connected with the two-story parking garage. Jonathan and Jessie were walking by the right railing.

"Hey, Mr. Science!" Rusty yelled. "Remember me?"

When Jonathan heard someone yelling, he whirled toward the building. *Rusty?* He blinked.

Jessie gasped. "You're supposed to be at the principal's office!"

"Who do you think I came over with?" Rusty approached, grinning. "Mr. Phipps is here to stop the field trip." He clenched his fists. "You ready to settle things, Park?"

Jessie put her hands on her hips. "Rusty, you're going to be stuck at the principal's office again *next* Saturday, too."

"Big whoop. I'm starting to like Mr. Phipps. He tells cool stories. So now what you gonna do, Park? No teacher to come save your hide this time."

Jonathan's stomach felt completely empty, except perhaps for a few dangling intestines. "I'm not afraid of you," he said.

"Then fight." Rusty swiped his fist in front of Jonathan's nose.

Jonathan stepped back. "I'm a Christian. Christians don't start fights just to fight."

THE CLUE FROM NINEVEH

Rusty sneered. "Are Christians chicken?"

"He's not chicken," Jessie said. "He's trying to obey God and love his enemy."

Jonathan thought about this. *That's true, that's what I should be doing.* He took a long breath.

"Look, Rusty. We've both been needling each other, and it's wrong. I'm willing to stop. I'm also willing to ask forgiveness for the wrong things I've done." He put his hand out. "Shake?"

"How 'bout this?" Rusty leaned closer and spit into Jonathan's outstretched hand.

Jonathan swallowed his disgust and wiped the wet glob off on his jeans. "I'm going to ignore that."

"Man, you're even more *spineless* than I thought. How about if I pick on your little friend?" Rusty stepped toward Jessie.

"Leave her alone!" Jonathan said.

Rusty sidestepped him and yanked Jessie's hair.

"Ow!" Jessie screamed. "Get away from me!"

Jonathan grabbed Jessie's arm and pulled her behind him. He wanted to squeeze Rusty's neck.

"I said leave her alone."

Rusty waggled his head. "Make me."

Jessie grabbed Jonathan's shoulder, trying to pull him away. "Stop it, guys! We're here to enjoy the museum, not to fight."

"Sorry, Jessie, but I'm tired of him bullying people."

"Ooh!" Rusty jumped back in mock fear. "Tough guy!"

"Can't you two be friends?" Jessie asked.

Rusty sneered. "I don't need a 'Too Good For Everybody Else' for a friend."

Rusty started circling. Jonathan forced himself to breathe through his mouth, hoping the oxygen would steady his racing brain. He also turned, keeping between Rusty and Jessie. Rusty paused with his back to the railing. He raised his fists.

Jonathan tapped his foot, still trying to stay calm. "Rusty, are you going to leave Jessie alone and quit picking on my friends?"

"No, I'm going to settle things with you!" Rusty swung.

The wind popped out of Jonathan's lungs and he doubled over, his stomach feeling flat as a pancake. Rusty poised another fist.

Jonathan lunged, hoping to grab the bully's waist and knock him to the ground. Instead, Rusty spun, and Jonathan slammed into the railing. Something cracked—suddenly there was no railing stopping him, only empty air. He felt like he was floating above a big dark asphalt blur. Then his fingers scraped something metal and he clung.

Jessie screamed.

Jonathan's legs swung free, his whole weight dangling from his hands. A piece of railing had cracked off and he was holding on to a bent piece of piping. There was no crossbar—only slick metal that thinned into nothing.

"Jessie—I'm—slipping," Jonathan gasped.

"Hold on!"

"I didn't mean to knock him through the railing!" Rusty's voice dripped fear.

Jessie grabbed Jonathan's knuckles, but she was too light to pull him up.

"Help him, Rusty! You're stronger."

"N-no way. I'm out of here." Rusty's feet scraped on the cement, then clattered toward the museum.

"Jessie, get someone else!" Jonathan said. "I don't know how long I can hold on!"

His weight kept pulling him down, inch by inch, toward the end of the pipe. *God, help me!*

Back inside the museum, Dr. Park was still lecturing. He had moved on from the seal and was leading the way around some of the other exhibits, still waiting for Jonathan to come back with the translation of the Sumerian account. It was taking much longer than Dr. Park expected.

He had asked for examples about things that looked good in nature. Sunsets, seashores, snow-capped mountains—the list was typical.

"Now," Dr. Park said, are there things in nature that aren't so good?"

Elizabeth's hand went up. "Hurricanes!"

"Very good. Yes, Eddie?"

"Famines and droughts."

"And diseases!" Thad said. "People die."

Dr. Park nodded. "Excellent examples. So in this world we see good things in nature and bad things in nature. Could it be that the world was once a perfect place that was invaded by evil and death?" He paused next to a display about ancient battles. "Genesis explains all of this. It teaches us that when Adam and Eve disobeyed God, paradise was indeed invaded by evil. It fits perfectly with the Bible."

Mr. Benefucio had been looking more and more puzzled as Kendall talked. Now, he raised his own hand, as if he were one of the children.

"Wouldn't God be cruel to allow evil to overcome the world?"

"Cruel by whose standard? God determines what is right and wrong, not man. Because man sinned against God, we deserve punishment. Amazingly, God has given us a road back to paradise—forgiveness through His Son, Jesus Christ."

Somewhere down the hallway a door slammed and footsteps clattered toward the traveling exhibit room. Jessie rounded the corner.

For a second, Dr. Park was shocked to see her running in the museum. Then he saw her face. Something was wrong.

"Dr. Park, Jonathan fell over the railing!"

Adrenaline spiked through Dr. Park's veins. He ran toward Jessie.

"What's happened?"

Jessie headed for the stairs to the outside. She was panting. "Rusty—and Jonathan—the railing broke."

Dr. Park flung through the double-doors that led to an open cement bridge to the parking garage. Iron railings lined both sides, except for one gap on the right where there was no railing. A man he didn't recognize was laying on the cement, his hands wrapped around the legs of a boy. The boy had red hair—it wasn't Jonathan.

After Jessie left, Jonathan kept praying and gripping with all his might. He tried to hold his body as stiff as he could, because every wiggle made him slide farther toward the end of the pipe. The veins running from his wrist to his elbow bulged in a sickening blue maze.

"Are you still there?" someone whispered.

"Yes!" Jonathan slipped another inch. "Help me!"

Rusty's head peered over the side. His eyes were wide. His lips twitched.

"Park, please, I'm sorry—"

"Rusty, help!"

The pipe creaked. Jonathan couldn't hold on any longer. He slipped toward the sharp pipe-edge and closed his eyes.

"Got you!"

Hands clasped his wrists and stopped his fall as the pipe slipped through the air. Jonathan clutched at the hands and locked his fingers with Rusty's.

"You're—heavy." Rusty grunted. He started lowering

Jonathan toward the ground.

"What are you doing?" Jonathan said. "I'm too high up!"

"My legs are slipping. I'm slipping, Park! I'm falling! Help!" Rusty yelled.

Footsteps pounded on the cement. "What's going on?" It was Principal Phipps. "That girl said someone fell. Rusty, what are you doing?"

"Help!" Rusty yelled again.

Jonathan was staring up at the sky, and for a second he saw Mr. Phipps' face framed through the railing. Then Rusty stopped slipping.

"I've got you, Rusty," Mr. Phipps said. "Now pull him up higher."

"My fingers—I can't hold on much longer!"

"Come on, do it, pull him up."

Jonathan felt Rusty's fingers weakening. His own were losing feeling after clenching the pipe so long. They felt like ten little bones poking upward.

"Rusty, you can't drop him," Mr. Phipps said. "You hear me? You're thinking it will look like an accident."

"I'm not!" Rusty screamed.

Rusty's hands jerked Jonathan up, then, as he hung suspended for a moment before plunging back down, strong hands grasped Jonathan's shoulders and pulled him over the edge. Jonathan groveled on the hot cement, his face pressed into the grit, tears of relief wetting his cheeks. *Thank you, God.*

"Jonathan!"

Dr. Park collapsed on the ground by his son's side, and hugged him tightly.

Someone was crying. Jonathan sat up, his head still giddy from the fright. He thought it was Jessie crying, but it wasn't— it was Rusty. He was sobbing into Mr. Phipps' shoulder, and Mr. Phipps' eyes were also wet as he bent over him.

"It's okay, kid. Everything's okay."

Dr. Park reached out his hand. "Mr. Phipps, I'm very much in your debt."

"Forget it." The principal cleared his throat and pulled Rusty to his feet. "About time one of us principals earned his pay. Jonathan, did Rusty push you over that railing?"

Jonathan shook his head. "No—not exactly. Truth is, sir, we've both been pretty mean to each other lately. I'm sorry, Dad. Rusty started picking on Jessie, and I couldn't let it go."

"He was fighting for me, Dr. Park," Jessie said.

Rusty wiped his nose on his sleeve. "If it makes any difference, Park, I didn't mean to knock you off."

"Thanks, Rusty. And you too, Mr. Phipps. I think you're a nice principal."

Mr. Phipps blinked. "Nice? Oh. Well—let's just say I'm a nicer principal today than I was yesterday."

"Sounds like you had quite an adventure in the museum."

"It was." Lou Phipps was walking on the path outside of the school so that no one could hear his conversation. "Yeah, Barry, it was, but that's not why I'm calling. You keep trying to change the subject."

"All right, Lou. What's the catch?"

"No catch. I'm giving you back every cent I blackmailed you out of." There was silence on the other end. Mr. Phipps chuckled. "Barry, you still there?"

"Yeah. Yeah—all right—and the other money?"

"Other money?" Mr. Phipps asked. "Oh, you mean the money *you* stole. Relax, Barry. I'm giving that back too."

"What do you mean *you're* giving it back?"

"I mean that I'm making a special donation to the school district."

"And just what do you hope to accomplish?"

Mr. Phipps stopped walking. That was a good question. One that had stumped him. "I guess—I guess so that I can look at myself in the mirror again."

"But you don't have that kind of income. How can you afford it?"

Mr. Phipps smiled a little bitterly at the bushes. "I can't, really. You can help me out if you want. Otherwise, I'll take out a loan."

"Have you lost your mind?" Mr. Brussell still sounded shocked. Mr. Phipps imagined him sitting in his office, his eyes as round as quarters. Either that, or they were squinted nearly shut with suspicion. "What do you expect me to say?" Mr. Brussell asked.

"Well, how about 'wow, Lou! What a nice person you turned out to be.' Something along those lines, maybe?"

"Quite frankly, your change of heart concerns me. Usually people with a change of heart start talking."

"I'm not quite ready to incriminate myself," Mr. Phipps said. "Now, I can't promise what will happen if they ever take a closer look at our books. However, in the meantime, you won't have any trouble from me."

"Lou? Seriously—what happened?"

Mr. Phipps picked up a stick with his free hand and poked at a bunch of dead leaves in the bushes.

"Somebody called me a nice principal. I liked the sound of it, but it was a title I wasn't living up to. I've kind of gotten re-acquainted with my conscience. I've even—" Mr. Phipps gulped. "I've even started thinking about God."

On Monday, the news came from Mr. Benefucio. Mr.

Phipps was going to overlook the museum incident. Jonathan was ecstatic.

"I've talked with Mr. Phipps a couple times at school. He seems like a different person." Jonathan grabbed another cookie from the fresh plate on the counter.

"A person in the process of being called by God, I would suggest," Grandpa Benjamin said.

Jessie tsk-tsked as Jonathan reached for a third cookie. "I just wish Rusty were a different person," she said.

Jonathan agreed. "At least he hasn't been quite as bad since the museum. I think it scared him."

Grandpa Benjamin leaned on the counter. "Well, Jonathan, now what do you think about God's command to love your enemies? Can you see the good that came out of obeying God, even when you didn't completely understand?"

"I think so, Grandpa."

Mrs. Park lifted the last plate of cookies from the oven and slipped out of her oven mitts. "It may affect Rusty some day too. His story isn't over."

"The important thing," Dr. Park said, "is that you did what was right, Son. That's its own reward."

Once the cookies were devoured, everyone split up, and Jonathan and Jessie headed for the living room.

"Jonathan," Jessie said, "thanks for watching out for me in the museum."

"No problem." Jonathan grinned. "That's what I'm here for."

The Adventure Continues!

Read *Jonathan Park: Return to the Hidden Cave*

Study Questions

The Clue from Nineveh
(Answers are on page 168)

1. What did Jonathan do in his classroom to showcase a "miracle" of science?

   _____

2. Is the DNA code enough information to explain a chameleon's ability to change color?

   _____

   _____

3. What does the verse Romans 8:28 say?

   _____

   _____

4. Give the TWO reasons why Grandpa Benjamin shared the verse above.

   _____

   _____

   _____

   _____

5. What is another name for microevolution?

   _____

6. How is macroevolution defined?

   _____

   _____

7. What is an example of observed macroevolution?

   _____

   _____

8. What was Dr. Park's point about proving the existence of Australia as it relates to proving the existence of God?

   _____

   _____

   _____

   _____

9. What proof do we have of a God?

   _____

   _____

10. What scene is most likely represented on the Greenstone Cylinder?

    _____

    _____

11. What was the other example Dr. Park shared in conjunction with the Greenstone Cylinder?

    _____

    _____

12. What was Dr. Park's point of sharing accounts of Genesis from artifacts and stories?

    _____

    _____

    _____

    _____

13. How does Dr. Park answer the question, "Wouldn't God be cruel to allow evil to overcome the world?"

    _____

    _____

    _____

    _____

Questions with Answers

Disaster at Brenan Bluff

1. What scientist did Grandpa Benjamin say was most likely a Christian and offered this quote to confirm: "this most beautiful system of the sun, planets, and comets could only proceed from the counsel and dominion of an intelligent and powerful Being.'?

   Isaac Newton

2. Name at least one of Isaac Newton's accomplishments as mentioned in the story?

   Developed calculus, invented the first reflecting telescope, studied the motions of our solar system and discovered of gravity.

3. What did Louis Pasteur invent?

   He invented the process we call 'pasteurization,' or the process that takes harmful bacteria out of milk.

4. What did some of Pasteur's important experiments prove?

   He did a series of experiments that proved the scientific law that says that life can only come from life.

5. Finish Pasteur's statement: "the more I study nature, the more _____."

   "I stand amazed at the work of the Creator"

6. Why did Mrs. Park quote Proverbs 16:18, "Pride goes before destruction, and a haughty spirit before a fall," to Jonathan?

   Jonathan was bragging about going on the radio talk show and offended some of the boys.

7. Who was John Woodward and when did he live?

   A creationist paleontologists who lived in the 1600s.

8. What did John Woodward believe?

   He believed the reason for so many fossils in the ground was a direct result of Noah's Flood. Just like the fictional dinosaur graveyard on Brenan Ranch—it shows evidence of a great flood.

9. Name one of the real-life scientists interviewed on the radio program.

   Dr. John Baumgardner (Ph.D. in geophysics at Los Alamos National Laboratory) or
   Dr. Russ Humphreys (physicist at Sandia National Laboratories) or
   Dr. Danny Faulkner (Ph.D. in astronomy, professor at the University of South Carolina, Lancaster) or
   Dr. Otto Berg (astrophysics, NASA) or
   Dr. John Morris (president of the Institute for Creation Research) or
   Dr. DeYoung (chairman of the Department of Physical Science at Grace College, Winona Lake, Indiana, faculty member of the Institute for Creation Research)

10. What did Dr. John Baumgardner, scientist with the Los Alamos National Laboratory, create on a computer?

    A model of a large tectonic catastrophe he is persuaded completely resurfaced the planet Earth in a very short period of time.

11. What inventor said, "I find it as difficult to understand a scientist who does not acknowledge the presence of a superior rationality behind the existence of the universe as it is to comprehend a theologian who would deny the advances of science"?

    Wernher von Braun, the man who designed the rocket that put a man on the moon.

African Safari

1. What was Dr. Cassat really interested in digging up?

   Uranium-235

2. What Bible verse says, "Be anxious for nothing, but in everything by prayer and supplication, with thanksgiving, let your requests be made known to God; and the peace of God, which surpasses all understanding, will guard your hearts and minds through Christ Jesus." ?

   Philippians 4:6

3. Why did Grandpa Benjamin share Philippians 4:6 with Dr. Park?

   Dr. Park was feeling down about the lack of money they had to build the creation museum and he was questioning if they would be able to build it at all.

4. What kind of fossil did Dr. Benson tell Dr. Park they were recovering? What is the name of one of the most famous fossils of this kind?

   Australopithecus afarensis. Lucy.

5. How does Dr. Park answer Dr. Benson's question, "how do you reconcile the ape-man fossils?"

    They fall into two categories: either they are within the range for modern humans, or they have traits similar to apes or chimps.

6. Name the two "false findings" of half-man and half-ape that Dr. Park mentioned.

    Neanderthal and Ramapithecus

7. What was the main reason that Dr. Benson suggested that "Ethel" was a hominid?

    The hip indicated an animal capable of walking upright like a human.

8. What was Dr. Park's reply to Dr. Benson's reasoning?

    Ethel would have walked, somewhat upright, like Pygmy chimps. Dr. Park saw an extinct created ape-like animal. Not an evolved form.

Escape from Utopia

1. What did Frank Drake do in 1960?

   Listened to the sky on a radio telescope for proof of extra terrestrial intelligence.

2. What does SETI stand for and what is the new name of the project?

   The Search for Extra-Terrestrial Intelligence. Project Phoenix.

3. What example did Dr. Park use to show how random chance could not create the universe?

   Dr. Park described how many combinations just eighteen people standing in a line can make—6 quadrillion, 400 trillion different line combinations. It takes 400 amino acids lined up to make just one protein and 60,000 proteins to make one cell. A human body is made up of trillions of cells!

4. How did Jonathan answer the question, "What if life evolved somewhere else, and then was brought to planet Earth?" and "Who created the creator?"

   Jonathan responded: "You're just transferring the problem somewhere else. Life is too complex...there's no way to explain it but by a Creator. The Bible talks about the Creator who has always existed. He's the One who planted life here on Earth, and He told us how. And, He made humans in His image."

5. What is the main problem of believing God created people on other planets? What does Romans 8:22 have to do with this?

    Romans says, "For we know that the whole creation groans and labors with birth pangs together until now." If there are other people on other planets, were they cursed because of what we did on Earth? If there were all kinds of other worlds with other people, did Jesus have to go from planet to planet, dying for each one?

6. How did Mrs. Park answer Katie's question, "So why did God make the universe so big, if there isn't anyone else living there?"

    "I think God is the divine Artist who created this big universe simply because He likes to create—like a painter, who hides things in his paintings he knows no one else will see. He does it just for His own good pleasure."

7. Beside Earth, are their plantets found which could support life?

    No.

The Clue from Nineveh

1. What did Jonathan do in his classroom to showcase a "miracle" of science?

   He had a chameleon change color based on its environment.

2. Is the DNA code enough information to explain a chameleon's ability to change color?

   No. Jonathan said, "We know the lizard has it in his DNA, and we know what it does, but we can't explain why the DNA programs it for protection. Not without God, we can't. A program needs a programmer."

3. What does the verse Romans 8:28 say?

   "And we know that all things work together for good to those who love God, to those who are the called according to His purpose."

4. Give the TWO reasons why Grandpa Benjamin shared the verse above.

   He shared this because Jonathan's presentation was used by God to bring Dr. Park into the class and it was the means of eventual reconciliation between Jonathan and Rusty.

5. What is another name for microevolution?

    Adaptation.

6. How is macroevolution defined?

    One kind of animal changing into another kind of animal.

7. What is an example of observed macroevolution?

    There are none. Evolution from one species to another has never been proven.

8. What was Dr. Park's point about proving the existence of Australia as it relates to proving the existence of God?

    None of the children in the class could prove that Australia exists, but the evidence for Australia's existence is so enormous and obvious that they accept it.

9. What proof do we have of a God?

    We have the witness of nature itself. Every design must have a designer.

10. What scene is most likely represented on the Greenstone Cylinder?

The Garden of Eden story found in Genesis.

11. What was the other example Dr. Park shared in conjunction with the Greenstone Cylinder?

The Sumerian account of the land of Dilmun, a land of perfection with no pain or disease.

12. What was Dr. Park's point of sharing accounts of Genesis from artifacts and stories?

"If the Bible is really true, then all nations and people are descended from Adam and Eve. The history of these events would be handed down by each nation. Some of the details might have changed, as each culture exaggerated and perverted the exact retelling, but the basic story would remain the same."

13. How does Dr. Park answer the question, "Wouldn't God be cruel to allow evil to overcome the world?"

"Cruel by whose standard? God determines what is right and wrong, not man. Because man sinned against God, we deserve punishment. Amazingly, God has given his elect a road back to paradise—forgiveness through His Son, Jesus Christ."

CPSIA information can be obtained at www.ICGtesting.com
Printed in the USA
BVOW09s2008261114

376582BV00002B/2/P